# GRIZZLY!

His fear getting the better of his reason, Nathaniel instinctively backed away from the bear, retreating into the shallow water at the edge of the river.

The grizzly dropped onto all fours and advanced ponderously, rumbling deep in its chest, its eyes fixed on the man.

Nathaniel could stand the strain no longer. He cupped his hands to his mouth and bellowed at the top of his lungs, "Zeke! A grizzly!" Then he retreated several more strides.

The shout prompted the grizzly to growl louder, and it stepped to the river's edge, then hesitated for a moment.

Nathaniel glanced over the bear's back, and his hopes soared when he spotted his uncle sprinting toward the bear, a rifle in each hand. He began to think he would survive his first encounter with a grizzly without receiving so much as a scratch, that perhaps the reputation of the species for ferocity was vastly overestimated, when the bear proved him wrong.

The grizzly attacked.

# WILDERNESS

## King of the Mountain

**David Thompson**

LEISURE BOOKS     NEW YORK CITY

**Dedicated to . . .**
**Judy, Joshua, and Shane.**

**To the memory of Joseph Walker,**
**Jedediah Smith, Jim Bridger,**
**and the rest.**

**Oh. And to Roland Kari.**
**We were born about a century too late.**
**We missed out on all the fun.**

A LEISURE BOOK®

September 1990

Published by

Dorchester Publishing Co., Inc.
276 Fifth Avenue
New York, NY 10001

# HISTORICAL NOTE

This book is as factually oriented as is humanly possible. Contemporary narratives of trappers, mountain men, fur traders and other archives were consulted to ensure authenticity. Certain fictional liberties have been taken in the interests of dramatic licence, which I hope the reader will agree contributes to the excitement of actually "being there."

From the records and evidence available, it is believed that the King cabin was located in what is now known as Estes Park, Colorado, just outside of Rocky Mountain National Park.

The Author

# Chapter One

"Out of the way, you dunderhead!"

The harsh bellow made 19-year-old Nathaniel King glance up and to his left; his green eyes widened in alarm. A moment before he had started to cross the narrow cobblestone street. Now he darted back to safety as a speeding carriage rushed past, narrowly missing him, the breeze from its passage stirring his moderately long black hair.

Cackling crazily, the driver of the carriage looked over his left shoulder and waved his whip in the air, apparently deriving perverse pleasure from almost running a pedestrian over.

An impulse to chase down the fellow and thrash him soundly compelled Nathaniel to take several strides after the rapidly departing brougham, and only the realization that he would be late for work prevented him from racing in pursuit. Instead, he drew his heavy wool overcoat tight about him to ward off the chill in the January air, and continued on his way to the accounting firm of P. Tuttle and Sons.

Located several blocks to the north of the New York Stock Exchange, in a stately sandstone bearing a huge sign comparable in size to the owner's view of his own importance to the business community, P. Tuttle and Sons seemed to exist at the center of a swirling vortex of humanity. Passersby streamed past the front window, while an increasing parade of carriages and buggies, wagons and gigs swept past going in either direction. The perpetual clatter of hooves and the hubbub of conversation, punctuated by whinnies and occasional oaths, lent the scene the aspect of a madhouse.

Or so Nathaniel often thought, and he did so now as he paused to gaze at the noisy street. He took one last breath of sooty New York air, then squared his broad shoulders and opened the door.

"My stars! Can it be that young Master King has finally graced us with his presence?"

The sarcastic comment drew Nathaniel around to his right, and he mustered a smile at the sight of his employer, Percival Tuttle the Elder, standing a yard away holding his open watch in his gnarled right hand. "Good morning, Mr. Tuttle."

"Is it really?" Tuttle responded wryly. "And here I thought it might be closer to noon."

"I'm sorry if I'm late."

"Late, Mr. King? No, I wouldn't go so far as to label you late. Tardy, yes. Tardy two days out of every month. Why, I will never know. Not when you only have two miles to travel to work. Yet I know my watch is accurate, and by my watch it is three minutes past eight."

"I'm truly sorry," Nathaniel said, self-conscious of the stares of the other employees, particularly Matthew Brown, Mr. Tuttle's pet.

"If I had a dollar for every time you have said you were sorry, I'd be a rich man," Tuttle the Elder declared dramatically, and snapped his watch case shut. "Fortunately, Mr. King, I practice the Christian forbearance instilled in me by my sainted mother. I forgive you for not arriving on time. For all your tardiness, you're a hard worker. I'll grant you that much."

"Thank you, sir," Nathaniel said dutifully, and hurried to his desk situated against the right-hand wall, near the window.

"There is one thing that worries me, though," Tuttle mentioned almost as an afterthought, although he deliberately raised his voice to attract the attention of the other seven employees.

Nathaniel began to shrug out of his overcoat. "What might that be, sir?"

An impish gleam came into the white-haired gentleman's brown eyes. "If you persist in failing to be on time when you are a bachelor, when you have no responsibilities other than yourself, I shudder to think how tardy you will be after you have acquired a wife and family."

A hearty burst of laughter greeted the remark.

As he had done so many times in the past, Nathaniel smiled to acknowledge Tuttle's profound insight and wit, then draped his coat on one of the wooden pegs in the corner.

"You will, of course, stay six minutes extra this evening to make amends," Tuttle stated.

"Of course," Nathaniel said.

Tuttle uttered a protracted sigh. "When I agreed to hire you as a favor to your father, my dear and loyal friend, I had no notion of the challenge you would present." So saying, he wheeled and walked off to his office.

Nathaniel sat down and considered the mountain of work piled in the middle of his desk. A snicker came from his left, from the plump person of Matthew Brown, and Nathaniel shifted to regard his corpulent rival critically. Brown's desk, in contrast to his own, was as neat as a spinster's dress. "Don't start, Matt," he warned.

Brown ignored the admonishment. "Won't you ever learn, Nate?"

"I've learned enough to know when to mind my own business," Nathaniel assured him, and opened the top file on his pile.

"Irritable today, are we?"

"I have work to do."

"I'm all caught up on mine. I'll help you if you wish," Brown said. He was—unfortunately, as far as Nathaniel was concerned—a mathematical genius.

"No." Nathaniel brushed some lint from his checkered trousers, wishing he were as adept as Matt Brown.

"Why won't you ever allow me to assist you?" Brown asked, his tone implying his feelings had been hurt.

"I'll do my own work, thank you."

"Has anyone ever informed you that you're pigheaded?" Nathaniel's eyes flashed up from the profit-and-loss statement he had started to study. "Have a care, Matt. I won't take that type of abuse from any man."

"Oh, mercy!" Brown said, placing his right palm against his cheek. "I'm scared to death."

"Do your work and leave me alone," Nathaniel said, returning to the figures under his nose.

"Who are you trying to fool?" Brown persisted, whispering so as not to be overheard by the other employees. "You take abuse from Old Man Tuttle every day of the week except Sunday. Don't play tough with me. Who do you think you are, anyway? Jim Bowie?"

The mention of Bowie caused Nathaniel to lean back in his chair, reflecting on the newspaper article published in September of the previous year detailing the bloody duel between Jim Bowie and Major Morris Wright on a sandbar in the Mississippi River. For several weeks the fight had been the talk of the city. Any news of the frontier typically generated considerable excitement, and the battle on the sandbar had caused more than most.

Nathaniel recalled the details vividly. He read every book, story, and article on the west he could find, and his favorite pasttime was to daydream about the exciting exploits he had read about, the adventures of such famous figures as Bowie and Lewis and Clark. Contributing to his keen interest was the fact that his uncle had departed for the rugged, virtually unknown lands beyond the Mississippi a decade ago, and now lived somewhere in the Rocky Mountains.

"You'd better start pushing your pencil," Brown said. "Tuttle won't take kindly to you wasting his time."

"Mind your own business," Nathaniel said.

"Try prunes. I hear they do wonders for the temperament."

Nathaniel ignored the barb and diligently applied himself to his work. The morning hours seemed to drag by, and he had to resist the temptation to stare out the window at the bustling activity in the street. Tracking down an error in one ledger occupied most of his attention, and while running his right index finger down a column of figures he became aware that someone was hovering over his left shoulder. Startled, he glanced around.

"Hard at work, I see," the elder Tuttle said appreciatively. "Have you found the mistake in the Corben account yet?"

"Not yet, sir."

"Hmmmph. Well, you can take your midday break in thirty minutes."

"Thank you."

Tuttle went to leave, then halted and stuck his right hand in the pocket of his long-tailed black coat. "Oh. Before I forget, there is one more thing."

"Yes, sir?"

"Is there a reason you're having your mail delivered to this office instead of your father's house?"

"Sir?" Nathaniel said, puzzled by the question.

"This came for you two days ago, on Monday, and I misplaced it on my desk," Tuttle stated. From his pocket he withdrew an envelope.

"Who would be sending me mail here?" Nathaniel wondered aloud.

"You tell me," Tuttle replied, and handed the envelope over.

Nathaniel studied the scrawled handwriting on the front, noting the name and address of the sender, surprise and delight etching his features.

*Ezekiel King*
*Fort Leavenworth*

"A relative, I presume?" Tuttle queried, obviously having noted the name.

"My uncle," Nathaniel confirmed. "We haven't heard from him in eight or nine years."

"Why would he write you and not your father?"

"I have no idea."

"Well, advise him that as a general policy I do not accept personal correspondence at my business establishment. In this case, though, I'll make an exception."

"Thank you, sir."

"Just be sure to read it on your own time."

"Of course."

Tuttle nodded imperiously and headed for his office. It was a sanctuary that the employees were permitted to enter only on rare occasions.

Nathaniel deposited the letter in the top desk drawer and resumed working. He could scarcely concentrate on the numbers, his mind racing as he tried to deduce the motive behind his uncle's letter. Wait until his father heard the news! Aflame with curiosity, he became conscious of each passing second, and the next thirty minutes went by even more slowly than all the preceding hours. He grinned happily when Tuttle announced that he could take his break, and his fingers flew as he opened the envelope and spread the two crudely written pages on the desk. He began reading eagerly.

December 2, 1827

Dear Nate,

That you will be surprised at hearing from me, I have no doubt. Many a year and many a mile has come between us, and I hope you will still remember your old Uncle Zeke who let you ride on his back when you were a sprout, and who took you to the park on the Hudson River to play.

I'm mailing this to you at your place of employment rather than my brother's. Your Aunt Martha wrote me about your job last January. I don't want Tom to know I wrote you, so please don't tell him or there will be bad blood between us. Again.

Your father never did understand the reason I came out to the great West.

I expect to be in St. Louis in May of '28. Come there. I have found the greatest treasure in the world and I want to share it with you before I die.

You were always my favorite nephew.

If you decide to come, be at The Chouteau House on May 4. I'll be wearing the red so you know me.

Uncle Zeke

Nathaniel recoiled in stunned amazement at the last portion of the letter. He reread it again and again, marveling that his uncle would even think of asking him to travel all the way to St. Louis, to the very edge of the frontier, to the last major outpost of civilization, when his father and mother and two brothers were all in New York, when he had never been beyond Philadelphia, and when he had his career as an aspiring accountant to consider. The list of objections grew and grew. There was his sweetheart, Adeline, and his plan to eventually marry her and settle down in a house of his own.

How could his Uncle Zeke make such an insane proposal?

Dazed, Nathaniel sat back and mumbled, "Go to St. Louis? How in the—"

"What's that?" interrupted a familiar voice on his left.

Frowning, Nathaniel twisted and watched Matthew Brown take a bite from an overstuffed sandwich. "I wasn't talking to you."

"I distinctly heard you say something about going to St. Louis," Brown said, his mouth full, a sliver of beef dangling from the corner of his mouth.

"You were hearing things," Nathaniel insisted. He folded the letter, replaced it in the envelope, and struck them in the pocket of his Byronic-style coat.

"Are you planning to visit St. Louis?" Brown inquired.

"No."

"If you go, you're not in your right mind."

Annoyed, Nathaniel faced his coworker. "Is that a fact?"

"Certainly. Why would anyone want to leave the culture and refinement of New York for the barbaric society of St. Louis?"

"New York has its drawbacks too," Nathaniel said simply to be argumentative, although in his heart he agreed with Brown.

"Oh? What, for instance? Carriage congestion, pickpockets, footpads, and a little ash in your eyes in the winter when everyone has their fireplace lit? Such inconveniences pale into insignificance when you compare them to the benefits we enjoyed by living in the greatest city in the country, even the world."

"Now you're exaggerating."

"Am I? New York is the largest city in the United States. Do you realize there are one hundred and twenty-five thousand people living here? Why, there are only about ten million people in the whole country. Over one-tenth of the total population lives in New York State. Imagine that!"

Nathaniel gazed out the window at the bedlam in the street and found it easy to imagine.

"Look at what New York has to offer," Brown continued, still chewing as he talked. "There's the opera, museums, and the ballet. Our theaters are the envy of the civilized world. Our newspapers are quoted everywhere. Why, the *New York Evening Post,* the one that William Cullen Bryant edits, is read by the President. Our universities are nationally renowned. Face facts, Nate. New York City is the cultural center of America."

The smugness with which Brown maintained his assertion bothered Nathaniel, but he was at a loss to identify the reason. "St. Louis has benefits to offer," he said lamely.

Brown snorted and almost choked on his sandwich. "Are you jesting? All St. Louis has to offer are ruffians, Indians, and the prospect of having your throat slit."

Nathaniel regarded the fat little man coldly, thinking that Brown wasn't the only New Yorker he knew who seemed to take an inordinate pride in his city, as if New Yorkers were superior to everyone else by virtue of their birthplace. He realized suddenly he shared that snobbish attitude to a lesser extent. New York could boast a culture rivaled by few other cities, but did that culture truly transform its residents into better citizens, better people, then those raised in, say, Boston or New Orleans or even St. Louis? He saw Matthew Brown stuffing more food into that gaping mouth and shook his head.

Brown misconstrued the motion. "What? You doubt you'll have your throat slit if you venture to St. Louis? How can you be so naive? You're read about the frontier. You know what it's like."

"Do I?" Nathaniel wondered wistfully.

# Chapter Two

The street lamps were lit by the time Nathaniel bundled himself in his woolen overcoat and started for home. He had performed his work that day in a perfunctory fashion, unable to fully concentrate, his mind adrift with the implications of his uncle's letter. The traffic outside was every bit as bustling as it had been that morning. He turned to the right and flowed with the crowd.

One sentence kept repeating itself over and over, unbidden but irresistible: "*I have found the greatest treasure in the world and I want to share it with you.*" What on earth could Uncle Zeke mean? Nathaniel mused. What kind of treasure? Had Zeke found gold or silver? There were many rumors about legendary treasures to be found out west, so perhaps Zeke had stumbled on one of them.

The most persistent legend, a tale every schoolboy learned by heart, concerned the Seven Golden Cities of Cibola. They were said to contain great riches, wealth so great that no man could conceive of the magnitude of the fortune. The seven cities were reputed to exist somewhere in the vastness between the Mississippi River and the Pacific Ocean; they were said to be inhabited by a tribe of fierce Indians. The

Spanish had sent several expeditions to find the Golden Cities of Cibola more than two hundred years ago, but although the expeditions had failed, the legend lingered on.

If Zeke had found gold, wasn't it only logical to assume that he would want to share part of his wealth with someone in the King family? And who better to share the gold with than his favorite nephew? Or so Nathaniel reasoned, and the more he thought about it, the more convinced he became that his uncle *had* made a fortune, and now wanted to mend the rift that had branded Ezekiel the black sheep in the King clan.

Engrossed in his reflection, and eager to reach home, Nathaniel opted to take a shortcut through an alley, a shortcut he might normally take during the day but had never used at night. He was halfway through the gloomy alley, his hands plunged in his overcoat pockets to shield them from the cold, his eyes straining in the dim shadows, when someone stepped from a recessed doorway and blocked his path.

Nathaniel halted abruptly, surprised but not worried, confident his size alone, six feet plus two inches, would deter most pickpockets and robbers from bothering him. "Excuse me, sir, but you're blocking my path," he said.

"Your money or your life."

The gruff words, delivered with an air of impending menace, startled Nathaniel. He knew about the hundreds of robberies that took place in New York City each year, and about the scores of footpads who made their vile living by preying on the innocent and the unsuspecting, but this was happening to *him*, and the reality of his predicament took half a minute to sink in.

"Didn't you hear me, fool? I want your money or your life!" the man declared.

Still stunned, Nathaniel mechanically pulled his hands from his pockets, about to comply, when he detected the flashing gleam of a large knife reflected in the feeble light from an overhead window.

"Don't trifle with me, mister!" the robber warned. "Give me your money now!"

"Go to hell," Nathaniel blurted out, and spun. He saw

the mouth of the alley not ten yards away, and he sprinted toward the opening in the hope that his assailant would not pursue him into the busy street. But he managed only three strides before strong arms caught him from the rear, looping about his hips, and the next moment he crashed to the hard ground with the footpad on top.

Instantly Nathaniel rolled to the right, nearly upending the thief in the bargain. The man clung fast to his overcoat, though, and Nathaniel saw the knife arching toward his chest. He lunged, grasping the robber's right wrist in his left hand, checking the knife's descent, and was clenching his right hand to deliver a blow with his fist when iron fingers clamped on his throat.

The footpad was attempting to strangle him!

Nathaniel bucked and squirmed, but he failed to disarm his foe or dislodge the constricting fingers from his neck. He tried to knee his attacker in the spine, but his overcoat impeded his movements. Frustrated, desperate to break free, Nathaniel felt a surge of newfound power course through him at the thought of being slain by an anonymous thug in a filthy alley.

"Damn you!" the footpad hissed. "Die!"

"No!" Nathaniel roared, and amazed himself by coming up off the ground in a mighty heave of his steely legs. He hurled the robber as if the man were a rag doll instead of a two-hundred-pounder, flinging him against the wall.

The footpad grunted as he hit the bricks, then dropped to one knee.

His fists at the ready, Nathaniel closed in, but the man scrambled to the right, then rose and dashed toward the street. "Hold on!" Nathaniel yelled, and gave chase. Again the overcoat interfered, preventing him from attaining his top speed. He was able to stay within two strides of the robber, though, and both of them burst from the alley without bothering to verify if the way was clear.

Voicing a harsh oath, the footpad collided with another man and both went down.

Not about to allow his adversary to escape, Nathaniel pounced and pinned the thief, his arms around the man's chest.

"Here, here, now! What is this?" bellowed someone in an authoritative manner.

Nathaniel felt hands on his shoulders, and then both he and the footpad were hauled erect.

"Now what is the meaning of this?" demanded a burly constable, who pulled the two men apart and held them at arm's length.

"He tried to rob me!" Nathaniel exclaimed.

"I did not," the footpad responded sheepishly. Revealed in the glow of a nearby street lamp, he was a stout, unkempt man with oily black hair and beady eyes.

The constable released both of them and looked from one to the other. "Now who am I to believe?"

"He has a knife," Nathaniel stated angrily. "He nearly stabbed me."

Smiling sweetly, the robber held up both hands. Both empty hands. "Search me if you like," he said. "You'll find no knife on Bobby Peterson. I'm a man who dislikes violence."

"He's lying!" Nathaniel cried. "He attacked me in the alley."

"Attacked?" Peterson repeated in astonishment. "Why, all I did was bump into the lad in the dark, and the next thing I know he had pulled me to the ground and we were wrestling. I never attacked him."

Nathaniel started to raise his right fist.

"No you don't, son," the constable cautioned. "No more fighting, if you please. Now here I am, on my way home to my loving wife and a hot meal, and I see you two fighting like a pair of cocks. What am I to do with you?"

"But he tried to *rob* me," Nathaniel insisted.

"I just have your word for that, now don't I?" the constable said.

The implied insult staggered Nathaniel. "Don't you believe me?"

"Of course I do. But I can also see where an excitable young fellow such as yourself might, shall we say, jump to conclusions without sufficient evidence."

"This is incredible."

A friendly smile creased the constable's weathered visage. "I'll tell you what. Let's so through this from the beginning again. Then we'll look for the knife you say Peterson had. But let's hurry, shall we? I'm starving."

"And the constable didn't believe you?"

"No," Nathaniel related. "Not after he couldn't find the knife in the alley. He let us go." He paused and added scornfully, "But he did give the robber a warning that he would be on the lookout and if he ever found Peterson had violated the law, there would be the devil to pay."

Adeline Van Buren shook her head sadly, her lovely features downcast in commiseration for his ordeal, her blond hair bobbing as her head moved, her blue eyes fixed lovingly on his face. In accordance with the fashion of dress in vogue all along the eastern seaboard, she wore a dress patterned after the sophisticated Grecian-style clothing so enormously popular in England and France. Her yellow dress had a low neckline, but not *too* low, and a high waistline. She folded her slim hands on her lap and stared at his scuffed shoes and the dirt on his trousers.

Nathaniel noticed, and wished he had changed before coming to see her. He'd already overstepped the bounds of propriety by arriving on her doorstep at nine P.M., a late hour for any respectable man to be calling on any decent woman. Fortunately, her parents thought highly of him and trusted him alone with their daughter. Everyone knew they were planning to wed in a year.

"What did your father say when you told him?" Adeline asked.

"He wasn't home. My father has been working long hours at his construction business."

"I thought January is one of his slowest months, what with the cold weather and all."

"He's busy with the yearly inventory," Nathaniel explained, admiring the shapely contours of her neck and shoulders. "I told my mother, but she couldn't seem to understand why I was so angry over the affair." He sighed.

"That's when I decided to pay you a visit. I knew you would understand."

"I'm happy you came," Adeline said.

Her smile thrilled Nathaniel to the core of his being. He wanted so much to be able to hold her in his arms, to touch his lips to hers and smell the fragrant scent of her coiffured hair. Her beauty seemed almost angelic, and when the time came, he would gladly throw himself at her feet and plead for her hand in marriage. So far all they had done was discuss the prospect. Soon, very soon, he would tender the formal proposal.

"There is a matter we must talk about," Adeline stated. "I promised Papa I would mention this to you."

Nathaniel tensed. Her father, a prosperous merchant with three stores in New York City and one in Philadelphia, had always impressed him as being a stern, commanding figure. He counted as a blessing the fact her father and his were close friends. "Mention what?"

Adeline opened her mouth to speak, then developed a sudden interest in her painted fingernails. "How has Mr. Tuttle been treating you?"

"As well as can be expected," Nathaniel replied, perplexed by the question. What did Old Man Tuttle have to do with anything?

"My father went to see him."

Nathaniel's breath caught in his throat, and he couldn't have moved if the house was on fire. He blinked a few times, struggling to compose his emotions, bewildered by the revelation. "Whatever for?" he blurted out.

Adeline looked at him, her eyes radiating all the affection in the universe. "Are you happy working for Tuttle?"

"Happy? Well, I don't know. Contented, maybe. It's a stepping-stone in my career. One day I'll own my own accounting firm. You wait and see."

"And that will take a terribly long time, won't it?"

"Not terribly long. Five, perhaps seven years at the most."

"And what will your income be?"

Nathaniel shrugged. "Who can say? It all depends on how successful I am in attracting clients."

"Will you make as much as your father does?"

"Not that much, but enough for us to live comfortably," Nathaniel answered, feeling uneasy, troubled by the direction their conversation was taking.

"Will you make as much as my father does?"

"Of course not. His income is in the six figures."

"And how many figures will yours be?" Adeline inquired, trying a new tack. "Five?"

Nathaniel said nothing.

"Four?"

"Oh, definitely."

A fluttering sigh issued from her rosy lips. "Nate, I'm accustomed to living in the style my father has provided for me all of my life. We're not immensely wealthy, but we are well off. I like having servants to take care of the menial chores like cleaning and cooking." She studied him for a moment. "Will we be able to afford servants?"

Nathaniel felt strangely deflated, as if his chest had been punctured and all the breath expelled from his lungs. "No," he admitted.

"I see," Adeline said, each word expressed in clipped, precise English.

"I'm confused," Nathaniel admitted. "You've known for over a year about my line of work and you've never raised an objection. Why now all of a sudden?"

"This is not a sudden consideration on my part," Adeline replied. "I've simply been waiting for the proper moment."

"For what?"

"To ask you to go to work for my father."

Nathaniel sat bolt upright in his upholstered chair. "Your father?"

"Why not?" Adeline rejoined stiffly. "In five years you could be managing one of his stores and making ten times as much money as you could by being an accountant."

"Does *he* want me to work for him?"

"Certainly, silly. Why do you think Papa went to all the trouble of seeking out Mr. Tuttle?"

"Why did he?"

Adeline gave him her most radiant smile. "I asked Papa

to do it. He had a long talk with your employer about your career as an accountant."

"And?"

"And we decided you would be better off joining Papa in his business."

"*You* decided?"

"Certainly. Don't I have a right to be concerned about your career? As your wife, the amount of money you make will have a direct bearing on my happiness and well-being. I have a vested interest in your future."

"But I like accounting," Nathaniel said softly, gazing absently at the plush lavender carpet, dazed by the unexpected turn of events. First the footpad, and now this. He should have known the day would turn out badly after almost being run over on his way to work. There was an omen, if ever there was one.

"Do you?" Adeline replied. "I know you *think* you do, but I have my doubts, dearest. I don't believe you have the proper temperament to be an accountant, to sit behind a desk the rest of your life and fiddle with figures. You have a restless nature, Nate King. You need excitement in your life, and retailing is just the thing to keep you from becoming bored."

"This is all so sudden," Nathaniel complained.

"You do see my point, don't you?"

Nathaniel nodded. "I see that money matters much more to you than I thought it did."

"Is that bad?"

"I suppose not," Nathaniel responded halfheartedly.

Adeline straightened and regarded him in the same manner a mother would a misbehaving child. "My father taught me a valuable lesson at a very early age, Nate. As he likes to say, money makes the world go around. Money, darling, is the balm of our existence. Money feeds us and clothes us and provides the pleasures we enjoy. Money separates the superior from the mediocre, and hard workers from the lazy riffraff." She paused. "I would never marry a man who was content to drift through life barely making ends meet. A man who will settle for making less than the highest income possible isn't much of a man in my estimation."

Nathaniel's lips barely moved when he said, "I had no idea."

"So will you give Papa's offer serious consideration?" Adeline inquired eagerly.

"For you, yes."

An airy laugh bubbled from her throat. "I knew I could rely on your good judgment. Why do you think I want to be your wife?"

The question drew Nathaniel's head up. "Why do you?"

"What a silly thing to ask. Because I love you. Because you treat me wonderfully," Adeline detailed, and giggled. "And because you are the handsomeest man in all of New York."

"I knew there must be a sound reason."

"Please don't be upset with me. This is for your benefit, as well as mine."

Nathaniel stared at her, studying her exquisite, elegant form, his pulse quickening as always, regarding her as a prize for which he was willing to pay any price. His brow knit and his eyes narrowed, indicative of the intensity he applied to pondering the issue she had raised, and in his single-minded determination to please her he entertained a wild idea. "What would you say if I could make more money than your father, more money than you ever dreamed possible?"

"Whatever are you talking about?"

"How would you feel if I was rich beyond your wildest expectations?"

Puzzled, Adeline leaned in his direction. "How could you possibly become richer than Papa?"

"Don't you believe I can?"

Adeline laughed lightly and smoothed her dress. "Please, Nate, don't become carried away. I want you to make more money, yes, but we must be realistic about the amount you can make."

Nathaniel reached in his pocket and touched the letter from his Uncle Zeke. Smiling, he removed his hand. "And I tell you that within six months I'll have more money than we will need."

"You're serious?"

"As God is my witness, I would never jest about making you happy."

"And how will you accomplish this magical feat?"

Nathaniel started to reply, to explain about the letter and his belief concerning the treasure Ezekiel had found, until he realized she would never understand, would never attach any credibility to his uncle's claim. Even his own family would view Zeke's letter as the ravings of an eccentric. But he knew better. He remembered the many hours he had spent with his carefree, fun-loving uncle; he recalled the basic decency and honesty Ezekiel had always displayed; he recollected the confidence Zeke had instilled; and motivated by the same impulse that had prompted countless men down through the ages to embark on questionable enterprises, namely the love of a beautiful woman, he came to a momentous decision. In answer to her question he only smiled and said, "Wait and see. You'll be proud of me one day soon. Very soon."

# Chapter Three

Nathaniel departed New York City on April 1, intending to travel at a leisurely pace and enjoy "the adventure," as he thought of his trip, to the fullest. He had planned every detail of his departure carefully, and he rode away through New Jersey on a fine mare, with another horse laden with his supplies trailing, at eight A.M. in the morning, oblivious to the nip in the air, his spirits soaring.

The four months since his receipt of Ezekiel's letter had been spent eventfully. He had put aside every cent he could spare for the journey, and combined with the funds he had already accumulated during his employment at Tuttle's and earlier, he now carried the hefty sum of 273 dollars in his inner coat pocket. He had purchased a blue wool cap to keep his head warm, and gone to a tailor to have new wool trousers made, trousers with extra stitching to withstand the rigors of extended periods in the saddle. He had also purchased a new pair of black leather boots, the ultimate in footwear according to the kindly man who'd made them, guaranteed to hold up under the harshest weather.

Nathaniel told no one about his plans. He dropped hints to Adeline, arousing her curiosity to a feverish pitch, but to all her entreaties he would only say that he intended to make her one of the wealthiest women in New York.

Once he attempted to broach the subject of Uncle Zeke to his family at the dinner table. His father immediately announced that Ezekiel had forsaken them to go live in the wilds with savage Indians, and accordingly Zeke was not, and would never be, a proper topic for discussion in the King household. End of subject.

During the four months Nathaniel's emotional state fluctuated between firm resolve and insecure anxiety. Scores of times he told himself he was being a fool. Yet the thought of traveling to the frontier, of seeing his uncle again, and most importantly, of possibly sharing in the treasure Zeke had found, beckoned like an irresistible beacon. The excitement of the unknown also appealed to him, the prospect of encountering strange people and strange lands and having experiences he could one day relate to his children and his children's children. The adventure promised to be a once-in-a-lifetime enterprise and he wanted to make the most of it.

On the night before he left, he composed three letters by candlelight at the small desk in his room. The first was to his family, explaining about the letter from Zeke and expressing his regret for leaving secretly. He assured his father and mother that he loved them, and vowed to return by July at the very latest. The second letter went to his employer, thanking Tuttle for teaching him the fundamentals of accounting and apologizing for leaving the firm in the lurch on such short notice. He also suggested that Matthew Brown would be delighted to handle the pile of work he hadn't finished.

Without a doubt, the hardest letter for him to pen was the note to Adeline. Four pages long, he poured his heart out to her, professing his love repeatedly, and pledged to return at the earliest opportunity. Knowing his father would inform her father about Zeke, he went into great detail about Zeke's letter and his belief that his uncle had amassed a fortune, either in precious ore or by trapping, like John Jacob Astor.

Everyone in New York who could read knew Astor's story. An immigrant from Germany who came to New York

City when he was twenty years old, Astor went into the fur trade in 1787, founded his own company in 1808, and eventually acquired a monopoly of the trade south of the Canadian border. In the process he became a millionaire many times over and the richest man in America.

Toward the end of his letter to Adeline, after vowing his undying affection one more time, Nathaniel added the lines tht would haunt him in later years. "Everything I do, I do for you. Your happiness means more to me than my own, more than my life itself. For you I would risk all. For you I would do anything. If money is your heart's desire, then money you shall have. Think of me always for I will constantly be thinking about you. In three months I will return to ask for your hand in marriage, and I'll be counting every minute until then."

Nathaniel thought of those closing words again as he rode to the southwest from New York, hoping Adeline would cherish them in her heart until next they met. Brimming with youthful confidence, he inhaled the crisp air deep in his lungs and congratulated himself on selecting the Cumberland Road route instead of taking the Erie Canal.

The decision had been a difficult one.

Traveling westward via the Erie Canal had been his first choice. Completed only a few years ago, in October of 1825, the canal linked the Hudson River and Atlantic Ocean with the Great Lakes, providing a much-needed water route into the heart of the country. Three hundred and sixty-three miles long, the waterway was daily jammed with boats crowded with passengers or transporting freight, and there had already appeared editorials in several newspapers calling for the canal to be expanded. For only a cent and a half a mile, passengers traveled at the rate of a mile and a half an hour on heavy boats pulled by horses. The going was exceedingly slow, which proved to be the deciding factor in Nathaniel's decision.

By contrast, a traveler on the Cumberland Road—or Great National Pike, as many referred to it—could move at whatever pace was necessary. Begun in 1811 and funded primarily with Federal money, the road ran from Cumberland, Maryland, up over the mountains and across the south-western corner of Pennsylvania, Ohio, Indiana, and Illinois, where it terminated at the town of Vandalia, not more than 61 miles from St. Louis. Although not yet completely paved, thousands traveled its almost 600-mile length each month. Sixty feet wide where completed, the road included a center strip to separate the traffic flow.

Nathaniel opted for the National Pike because he could ride as many miles each day as he wanted, and he would be much closer to St. Louis at the end of the pike than he would if he took the Erie Canal. By following the many signs and sticking to the major roads, he reached Cumberland on the evening of the seventh day. With approximately a thousand miles to cover, he was not inclined to push his horses. Both animals had been purchased at a stable on the southwest outskirts of New York City, and the proprietor of the livery had also agreed, for a nominal fee, to store Nathaniel's gear until such time as the supplies were needed. Nathaniel had not dared hide any of his provisions in his room for fear of them being discovered.

Once on the National Pike, Nathaniel began to relax and truly enjoy his trip. Guilt had nagged at his mind the first five days, until he'd finally convinced himself that his course of action was justified. He found the people traveling on the Cumberland Road to be remarkably friendly. Back in New York, he had been lucky to receive a curt nod in response to a hello. But the farther west he went, the more amicable the people were.

All types of travelers used the pike. Those heading west formed a steadily flowing river of vibrantly optimistic humanity, the vast majority en route to a better life in a better area of the country, where the sweat of their brow would reap the reward of having their own land and their own house, where they could prosper and share in the budding American dream. Or so they hoped. There were travelers from all walks of life and almost every state in the East. They went on foot, or on horseback, or in carriages or wagons. Livestock mingled with the people, primarily cattle being driven to Eastern markets by drovers from the frontier.

Nathaniel reveled in the journey. He particularly liked the evenings, when he invariably stopped at one of the many comfortable inns lining the road to eat and rest for the night. The stops gave him the opportunity to associate with his fellow wayfarers. He met a farming family intent on starting anew in Missouri, a doctor from Philadelphia who had grown tired of the city life and longed for a change, and a missionary heading for the Old Southwest to "Christianize the Indians." All told, he talked to dozens of fellow wayfarers during the 27 days it took him to complete the trip.

Three incidents of note transpired, two of which he would never forget for as long as he lived.

The first incident occurred at an inn in eastern Ohio, a shoddy establishment where the food was undercooked, the bed uncomfortable, and the manager a slovenly sort who always seemed to have a handkerchief pressed to his nose. Nathaniell had pushed his plate aside halfway through the meal and headed for his room. As he placed his right foot onto the bottom step, the manager suddenly appeared at his left elbow.

"I say, young sir, would you care for some pie?"

"No, thank you," Nathaniel replied, and went up two steps.

"But it's freshly baked tart pie."

Nathaniel glanced at the man, surprised to note a certain anxiety in the set of his chubby features. "Thank you, but no. I have spent all day on the road and I would like to retire early."

"I'll throw in a free ale."

Although tempted, Nathaniel shook his head, bothered by a vague feeling of unease. "Good night, sir."

The manager gave a small bow and backed away, frowning.

Now what was all that about? Nathaniel wondered, and proceeded to the second floor and along the dim corridor. Two yards from his room he halted, amazed to behold his door hanging open several inches when he distinctly recalled locking it behind him earlier on his way down to eat. He eased to the jamb and peered inside.

Looming as a vague inky shadow in the dark room, a burly man was in the act of rifling through Nathaniel's possessions piled on the bed.

Without thinking, angered by the sight of the thief tossing his clothing about, Nathaniel shoved the door wide and blurted out, "You there! Hold it!"

But the thief had no intention of doing any such thing. Uttering a curse, the man spun and charged the doorway, barreling into Nathaniel and battering him aside.

Lunging with his left arm, Nathaniel succeeded in taking hold of the other man's coat. Before he could capitalize on the grip, however, the thief jerked to one side and wrenched loose, throwing Nathaniel off balance into the opposite wall. Nathaniel pushed erect and gave chase, yelling, "Stop, thief! Stop, thief!"

The man never looked back. He reached the stairs and bounded to the bottom, taking the steps four at a stride, then bolted out the entrance into the night.

His pulse pounding, Nathaniel followed to the front door, when he paused to scan the lawn beyond for the pilferer. The earth had swallowed the man whole, and the expanse of green grass mocked him with its emptiness.

"Hear, hear! What's the meaning of this uproar?" the manager demanded, hastening over from the desk.

"A man was in my room," Nathaniel responded, still infuriated, still surveying the lawn.

"What man?"

"A thief."

The manager, his tone laced with the venom of a cotton-mouth, snapped, "Not in my establishment, young man."

Nathaniel spun, even more incensed at having his word doubted. "Are you calling me a liar, sir?" He expected the manager to argue the point, but to his surprise the man did an abrupt reversal.

"Not at all. I would never impugn the integrity of one of my guests. If you say there was a gentleman in your room, then by all means there must have been someone in your room."

"He wasn't a gentleman."

"Is it possible another guest might have entered your room by mistake?"

"The man wasn't a guest. He was a thief."

"Was anything stolen?"

The question galvanized Nathaniel into action. He bounded up the stairs to his room and checked his personal belongings. To his immense relief, none of his possessions had been taken. As he finished folding his clothes he heard someone cough behind him and turned to discover the manager.

"I have checked the grounds and there is no sign of anyone who shouldn't be here."

"The thief is undoubtedly long gone by this time."

"Is anything missing?"

"No," Nathaniel said.

"Then no harm has been done," the manager commented. "In the future, though, I would advise you to lock your door. Inns are not farmhouses. I have no way of knowing what type of person may be taking a room for the night. Occasionally someone bad slips in."

"So I see."

"Well, if that will be all," the manager said, and gave another of his courteous little bows. He grinned, an oddly sinister twisting of his thick lips, and walked off.

Nathaniel promptly closed and locked the door, then checked to ensure the single window on the east wall was securely latched. Unnerved by the incident, he pushed the bed against the door and lay down fully clothed on his back, his head resting in his interlocked hands. He stared at the ceiling for over an hour, reviewing the episode from start to finish, and came to the conclusion he must pick the inns he stayed at with greater care in the future. The manager's behavior troubled him, although he couldn't determine precisely why. He slipped into a fitful sleep, and his last thought before he slept was that he should give serious consideration to obtaining a weapon.

The second incident took place a few miles east of Indianapolis, which had been designated the capital of Indiana only

seven years before. He stopped shortly after noon to give
the horse a rest and enjoy a light meal at a quaint inn packed
with other travelers. His dinner consisted of delicious baked
beans, which had been steeped with generous portions of pork
in a big pot left overnight in the ashes of the inn's fireplace,
as was the custom. After eating he went outside to enjoy the
fresh air and the warm sunshine, and it was then, as he
strolled toward the southeast corner of the building, that he
saw them. At first he mistook them for shadows, and not
until one moved did the shock of recognition stop him in his
tracks.

They were seated under the spreading branches of an
enormous maple tree, at the base of the trunk, their backs
leaning against the rough bole, partly ringing the giant
patriarch of the forest that had once claimed the land on which
the inn sat. There were four of them, each with his knees
drawn up against an emaciated chest, each with iron shackles
on their ankles. Their clothes were in tatters, and the grime
from many miles of travel caked their sweating black skins.
Two of the four wore beards; the other two were quite young,
barely out of their early teens.

Nathaniel noticed them when one of the young blacks lifted
a weary hand to lethargically scratch a bulbous nose. He
halted in astonishment 20 feet from the maple and gazed at
them in bewilderment, striving to fathom the reason for their
condition and the shackles. The oldest of the quartet turned
a lined visage toward him, regarding him with the blank eyes
of someone who had penetrated an inscrutable veil and who
now viewed the world as if from a vast distance. Somehow,
those vacant orbs also conveyed the indelible stamp of
incalculable inner torment and sadness commingled in a
singular countenance. Nathaniel looked, and felt an invisible,
frigid wind chill his spine.

"Hey, you want somethin', mister?"

The words, spoken in a peculiar, protracted drawl, came
from one of the six men who were lounging about a wagon
parked a dozen yards to the south of the tree. All six wore
homespun clothes. Several rifles had been propped against
the wagon, and the speaker wore a large hunting knife in

a brown leather sheath on his right hip.

"Why are those men in chains?" Nathaniel asked.

"What's the matter, boy? Ain't you never seen slaves before?" the speaker rejoined, prompting a cackle of mirth from his companions.

Nathaniel turned, noting the man's ragged blond hair, wispy blond mustache, and pale blue eyes. "They're slaves?"

"Escaped slaves, boy. All the way from Mississippi. As ignorant a bunch of niggers as you'd ever want to meet."

Nathaniel had seen many Negroes in New York, although in the circle of his acquaintances he could number only two Negroes he knew personally. Both had been slaves, domestic servants in the house of a man who did business with his father, and both had been freed on July 4, 1827 when the State of New York officially abolished slavery. The pair had stayed on with their former owner, apparently satisfied with the working conditions and the treatment they had received.

Many stories were related in the press about the growing institution of slavery in the Deep South, and the moral and legal aspects were vigorously debated. Other states besides New York, including Pennsylvania, Rhode Island, and the new state of Illinois, had banned the practice.

"Are those shackles necessary?" Nathaniel inquired distastefully.

"They are if we don't want them niggers to light out on us," the man responded. "We didn't trail 'em this far to lose 'em again."

"You're from Mississippi?"

"Yep. We do this for a living, and get paid fair money too. Slaves are always taking off, no matter how decent some of 'em are treated. They're so dumb it's pitiful."

Nathaniel looked at the oldest slave, who had tilted his head against the tree and closed his eyes. "Aren't there laws against chasing slaves across state lines?"

The blond snickered. "You sure don't know shucks about the slave trade, Yankee. Ain't you ever heard of the Fugitive Slave Law?"

The reference sparked a memory long buried, and

Nathaniel simply nodded. Back in 1793, or thereabouts, the Congress had passed the Federal Fugitive Law, which allowed slave owners to cross state lines if necessary to retrieve runaway slaves. He gave the quartet a last glance, then wheeled and hurried to the stable behind the inn to reclaim his horses, filled with an overwhelming urge to put as much distance as he could between the four chained human beings and himself. Until that moment, he had never seriously pondered the issue of slavery. For the remainder of the day he reflected on nothing else.

In Illinois, just over the border from Indiana, the third incident occurred.

Nathaniel stopped at an inn situated a little off the beaten path after he found two others, both nearer to the pike, full to capacity. He bedded his horses for the night, then took a room, washed, and ate a leisurely supper of tasty venison and potatoes. As he concluded the meal, he happened to gaze toward the rear of the dining area and spied an open door. Five men were visible in a room beyond, seated around a circular table, playing a game of cards. Intrigued, he rose, paid for his meal, and walked back to investigate. As he stepped through the doorway all eyes swung toward him. He halted, uncomfortable under their probing stares, wondering if he had committed a blunder by intruding on their game.

"What the hell do you want, whippersnapper?" demanded a bear of a man who wore a cape with a beaver-fur collar.

"I only wanted to watch," Nathaniel replied, putting as much self-confidence into his voice as he could muster.

"This isn't a church social. Go watch the birds play in the trees," the man snapped, and one of the other players tittered.

A third player then spoke, his tone firm, a slight edge to his pronouncement. "Leave him alone, Clancy."

Nathaniel focused on his defender, a slim man wearing an immaculate black suit and a frilled white shirt. The thin man's features were angular, his hair brown, his eyes an icy grayish-blue. He held his cards in his left hand, close to his shirt, while his right elbow rested on the edge of the table and his right hand was lost to view, evidently on his lap.

"Is this sprout a friend of yours, Tyler?" the man named Clancy inquired testily.

"Never laid eyes on the gentleman before," Tyler replied, smiling and nodding at Nathaniel.

"Then what difference does it make to you whether he stays or not?" Clancy demanded.

"If he wants to stay, he stays," Tyler stated with an air of finality, and locked his eyes on the bigger man.

Nathaniel saw the other men stiffen and lower their cards, and he glanced from Tyler to Clancy, noticing the obvious hatred gleaming in the massive man's dark eyes. Tyler sat calmly, composed and relaxed, but Clancy appeared on the verge of exploding into violence. A silent battle of wills had ensued, and neither man seemed willing to back down. Nathaniel inadvertently broke the deadlock by saying, "If I'm causing trouble, I'll be glad to leave."

"I don't give a damn whether you stay or not," Clancy said harshly, finally tearing his gaze from Tyler.

"Then let's play cards," another man said. "This constant bickering is ruining the game."

Nathaniel stood next to the right-hand wall and idly observed the course of the game. Having never been much of a card player himself, he still knew enough to recognize the five men were engaged in a form of poker. He watched as the cards were shuffled and dealt, listened as bids were made and coins tinkled on the table, and marveled at the intensity displayed on all the faces except one. Every player except Tyler sat in a posture of anxious expectancy and hung on the deal of each card. Curses were vented when hands went against them, and although they tried to conceal their elation when they received a good hand, most of them were transparent by their sudden silence or stony expression.

For over an hour the game continued. Tyler dominated the play, winning two out of every three hands, his pile of silver and gold coins and stack of paper dollars growing higher and higher. His slim, elegant hands handled the cards with balletic grace, his fingers flying when he dealt, gliding each card to the recipient with unerring accuracy.

Clancy became progressively surlier as he lost more and more money. Clearly an inept player, he insisted on challenging Tyler again and again. Each loss diminished his self-esteem and aroused his anger, and he began to cast open, spiteful glances at the man in black. He also started fiddling with his brown cape, moving the left flap from side to side. Despite the warmth, he kept the cape on, even though all of the other players had taken their coats off.

Nathaniel was about ready to retire and had stepped toward the doorway when the trouble began.

"Well, you've cleaned me out, Tyler," Clancy declared, throwing his last hand on the table in disgust.

"You play poorly," Tyler stated. He used only his left hand to rake in his winnings.

"You play well," Clancy responded, leaning forward. "Perhaps too well."

The other men suddenly pushed back from the table, giving Tyler and Clancy plenty of space.

"Be very careful."

"Don't threaten me, you dandy," Clancy spat. "I say you play too well."

Nathaniel could almost feel the tension in the room. The other players seemed scarcely to be breathing, as if they were waiting for a great and terrible event to transpire. They weren't to be disappointed.

Tyler placed his left arm on the table, a slow, deliberate, almost delicate gesture. His right hand was once again out of sight in his lap, a fact fraught with significance for all of the players except the irate Clancy, to whom he addressed his next words in a low, hard tone. "Say your meaning straight out."

"I say you cheat."

The players were now statues, rooted to their chairs, their unblinking eyes on the protagonists in the unfolding drama.

"You have insulted my integrity, sir, and I demand satisfaction," Tyler stated.

"I'll bet you do," Clancy said, and laughed, a short, brittle sound, an insult in itself.

"Name the time and the place."

Both thrilled and secretly appalled, Nathaniel listened to the challenge being issued in amazement. Tyler wanted a duel! He knew all about dueling, about the code of last resort for any offended gentleman, but he had never been privileged to witness one. Famous duelists were constantly making headlines. Only two years previously, Henry Clay and John Randolph had engaged in a much-publicized event. Clay, the Secretary of State, had challenged Senator Randolph after the latter had insulted Clay on the Senate floor. Their duel had prompted countless snide remarks and crude jokes because neither man had scored a hit. Clay had sent his shot through Randolph's coat, and the Senator had then elevated his pistol and fired into the air.

"Right here and now," Clancy replied angrily, rising to his full height.

"As the offended party, I claim the choice of weapons," Tyler said.

"Choose whatever you like. I'll be waiting outside," Clancy declared. He stalked from the room like a grizzly bear storming from its cave to do battle.

"Don't trust him, Adam," one of the other players remarked the moment Clancy was gone.

"No," chimed in another. "He's too treacherous."

Tyler stood, his forehead knit in thought. "Renfrew, will you kindly be my second?"

"Gladly, Adam," responded a white-haired man attired in a brown suit.

"My dueling pistols are in my room," Tyler said. "Would you fetch them for me?"

"Certainly." Renfrew hastily departed.

Tyler squared his shoulders and strode from the room, trailed by the remaining players, each man somber and reserved.

Enthralled, Nathaniel followed them, watching Tyler the entire time, marveling at the man's courage. The owner of the inn appeared and remonstrated with Tyler to call the duel off, but the man in black ignored the plea. The news was spreading rapidly, and patrons were flocking to the spacious green bordering the front of the establishment. As he emerged into the bright sunlight and squinted, Nathaniel spied Clancy waiting in the center of the green, standing next to his discarded cape, a large knife in a sheath in plain sight on his left hip.

Tyler waited for his second to return bearing a large black case, then both men walked out to Clancy.

Nathaniel moved through the crowd to obtain a clear view, and watched as Tyler and Clancy exchanged words. He wondered if Tyler was offering the big man a chance to select a second. Whatever the import, Clancy declined and pointed at the black case, saying something that made Tyler clench his fists in anger. The pistols were promptly distributed and the duelists aligned themselves back to back.

"This is horrible," a woman standing nearby remarked. "Someone should put a stop to this."

"If you believe it's horrible, don't look," advised a man dressed in breeches and a white shirt.

Nathaniel tried to take the measure of Clancy. The big man had impressed him as being an uncouth lout, but now he wasn't so positive. Clancy's clothes, while not as refined as Tyler's, were of good quality and clean, his black boots polished.

Renfrew carried the pistol case from the dueling field. He turned and called out, "At the count of three you will proceed ten paces, then face your opponent and fire."

Tyler and Clancy were immobile, each with his right hand next to his chest and his pistol pointing skyward.

"One," Renfrew cried.

A hush fell over the spectators, none of whom averted their eyes.

"Two."

A squirrel in an oak tree off to the right chitterred loudly, apparently peeved at all the noise.

"Three!" Renfrew shouted.

Transfixed by the tableau, Nathaniel saw the two duelists begin to pace. Tyler took measured treads, but Clancy moved swiftly, and the man in black had only gone eight steps when his adversary abruptly wheeled, raised his pistol, and fired.

The booming retort produced a cloud of gunsmoke, and simultaneous with the discharge Tyler stumbled forward as if slapped by an unseen hand. He recovered his balance, steadied himself, and pivoted.

Clancy took one look, saw his doom reflected in Tyler's visage, and threw the pistol to the grass. He whipped his knife from its sheath and charged, bellowing inarticulately at the top of his lungs, as if his maniacal yells could accomplish what his aim had not.

Tyler never hurried. He elevated his pistol slowly, he took aim slowly, and when Clancy had only five yards to cover, he squeezed the trigger slowly.

The ball struck Clancy squarely in the forehead and burst out the rear of his cranium, splattering blood and brains every which way, rocking the big man on his heels for a moment before he toppled over with an incredibly puzzled expression, as if his passage into eternity constituted a perplexing mystery.

Before Clancy hit the ground Renfrew and others were hastening to Tyler's side. After firing, the man in black doubled over and staggered, and he would have fallen if his second had not reached him and provided support.

"Disgusting," commented the matron who had offered the earlier observation.

Nathaniel glanced at her, surprised she had stayed to witness the duel. She gazed at the dead man for several seconds, smacked her lips distastefully, and hurried into the inn.

Renfrew and four others were transporting Tyler inside, holding him as still as they could. A bright red stain had formed on Tyler's shirt, a stain that was spreading.

Upset by the unjust outcome, Nathaniel looked at the man in black as the party passed him. Tyler's face was pale, but his eyes were alert and they focused on Nathaniel. A reassuring smile creased the man's thin lips, and then he was past and being carried inside.

"So much for Noah Clancy," remarked a bystander, an elderly man in the garb of a farmer.

"He always was a braggart and a bully," said another.

"Who wants to bury him?" asked a third.

"I will," offered the farmer. "He's not a fit sight for children to see with his brains oozing out like they are."

Nathaniel lingered at the inn for several hours, waiting to hear the prognosis of a doctor who had been urgently summoned from a small town close by. He listened to other patrons relating the duel again and again and again, disgusted by their callous disregard of the man who might be dying upstairs. All they were interested in were the gory details. He sat in a corner, drinking an ale, listening to them chatter, and came to the conclusion they were the worst flock of vultures he had ever seen.

Only when the doctor announced that Tyler would live did Nathaniel walk to the stable and collect his horses. In 20 minutes he was back on the road, his mind preoccupied with thoughts of dying and death, of justice and honor, and in such a frame of mind he finally arrived at his destination.

# Chapter Four

St. Louis.

In 1764 a pair of French fur traders established a trading post on the west bank of the Mississippi River, just to the south of its junction with another mighty river, the Missouri. One of the Frenchmen decided to name the post after Louis IX, a French king who was made a saint, and thus St. Louis had its humble beginnings.

Located in territory originally claimed by the Spanish, St. Louis officially came under French jurisdiction when Spain ceded the region to France.

The transfer gravely alarmed President Thomas Jefferson. The French made plans to send troops to take possession of the territory, and President Jefferson became worried that they would not honor the agreement the U.S. had worked out with Spain concerning the city of New Orleans far to the south. American farmers and trappers who lived west of the Appalachian Mountains shipped their produce and goods by river down to New Orleans. If the French refused to continue the arrangement, untold economic hardships would result.

President Jefferson sent a delegation to France under orders to make a reasonable offer to purchase New Orleans and the Floridas. When the delegation tendered their proposal, they were astounded by the reaction. The French not only agreed to sell New Orleans, but *all of the territory the Spaniards had ceded over*. So, for the sum of approximately $15 million, the United States doubled its size and acquired the city of St. Louis in 1803.

And what a city it was.

Despite all the news reports and stories Nathaniel had read about the frontier, he was unprepared for the raw, bustling scene that blossomed before his astonished eyes as he entered St. Louis on the morning of April 29. First to attract his attention were the scores of steamboats and barges on the Mississippi River, enough to almost rival the harbor of New York on any given day. Grogshops and dozens of taverns literally lined the waterfront area, and rivermen, fur trappers, wagoners, and other rowdy types mingled in reckless abandon twenty-four hours a day.

Rearing above the waterfront area were the private residences of the wealthy and not-so-wealthy, a curious mixture of French, American, and even Spanish architecture that gave the city a distinctive quality all its own. The French were still very much in evidence, with their regal homes, Canadian horses, and curious little carts.

As Nathaniel rode into the heart of the city, he was pleasantly surprised to discover there were several newspapers in operation. He even passed a bookstore, and promised himself he would pay it a visit soon. There were also a number of theaters where live plays were performed daily. All in all, St. Louis was not anything like he had expected the city would be.

The one element Nathaniel did find, and which he had anticipated, was the abundant presence of firearms and other weapons. Nearly every man carried either a rifle, a pistol, a knife, or a sword. The few who didn't appeared, by their clothing, to be upper-class city residents. Every frontiersman strolling the streets had his rifle and knife, as much a part of his attire as his buckskins. Nathaniel had encountered more and more firearms the farther west he traveled, and now they seemed as indispensable for survival as the air itself.

Then there were the Indians. Nathaniel had not expected to discover so many of the red men within the city limits, and not until the third day of his stay did he learn the reason. General William Clark, the same Clark who had journeyed with Meriwether Lewis to the Pacific Ocean and back, was now the Superintendent of Indian Affairs, and on a daily basis large delegations of Indians arrived to confer with him.

Nathaniel took a room at The Bradley Hostelry, and put up his animals at a stable. Once his belongings were safely locked in his room, he took to the streets and ambled until nightfall, drinking in the sights and sounds in the manner of a starved man falling upon a side of roast beef. He couldn't seem to get enough. There was a vibrant, dynamic, vigorous atmosphere to St. Louis that thrilled his soul and enchanted him beyond measure.

That night in his room, as he lay listening to the sounds coming through his open window, he thought of New York and compared the metropolis to St. Louis. The comparison bothered him because he decided he liked St. Louis better. Both were bustling beehives of human commerce, but St. Louis was endowed with a robust, undisciplined vitality New York City lacked. Perhaps, long ago, New York had possessed the same frontier-style nobility, the same raw passion for life exhibited by the denizens of St. Louis, but not anymore. The people in St. Louis were living life to the fullest; the people in New York merely going through the motions while waiting to be planted six feet under.

Nathaniel spent the next day much as he had the first, strolling through the city and familiarizing himself with the location of various establishments and parts of town. He found The Chouteau House, one of the premier hotels in all of St. Louis, and wondered why Zeke would want to meet him at such an expensive place. He opted to stay at The Bradley Hostelry to conserve his funds.

Several hours that afternoon were spent browsing through

the delightfully large collection of books lining the shelves at the bookstore. There were bibles, of course, and cookbooks galore. There was a copy of *The History of the Expedition of Captains Lewis and Clark,* edited by Nicholas Biddle, which he was almost tempted to buy. There was a reprint edition of John Marshall's *Life of George Washington* that he found interesting. But by far the books that fascinated him the most were those by James Fenimore Cooper. He had already read Cooper's *The Pioneers,* published in 1823, and enjoyed the tale of the frontiersman Natty Bumppo immensely. Now he found *The Pilot,* a sea novel, and joys of joys, the next novel in the Bumppo saga, *The Last of the Mohicans.* Billed as an outstanding romance of the wilds, the story actually depicted Leatherstocking, as Bumppo was known, at an earlier age, embroiled in battles with the Iroquois. Nathaniel purchased the book and returned to his room. That night he ate a hearty meal and retired early.

For three days Nathaniel spent the daylight hours venturing about St. Louis and the evening hours reading *The Last of the Mohicans.* He made the acquaintance of the owner of The Bradley Hostelry, and of several other folks staying there, and during casual conversations learned more particulars about St. Louis and its history. Mr. Bradley warned him to avoid the taverns and grogshops if he valued his life. St. Louis, it turned out, was infested with the same blight as New York. Cutthroats and thieves prowled the streets after dark. There had even been several kidnappings of affluent citizens, who were returned after a suitable ransom was paid. Nathaniel was astonished to learn that the city did not have a regular police force.

On the morning of May 4 he hurried to The Chouteau House and inquired about his uncle, but no one named Ezekiel King had taken a room. Disappointed, he walked about the general vicinity for several hours, then returned. Again the clerk at the desk informed him that his uncle had not arrived. Troubled by the fact he might have traveled so far for nothing, Nathaniel walked aimlessly until midday. He checked once more, and once again had his hopes dashed.

"You should call again at five o'clock," the desk clerk suggested. "Few travelers like to be on the road at night, and if your uncle intends to register today he'll probably be here by then."

"Thank you," Nathaniel responded. He returned to his room and finished his book, then paced nervously until half past four, reflecting on the consequences if Zeke should fail to show as promised. He winced at the mere thought of going back to New York City empty-handed, convinced he would become the laughingstock of his family. Not only that, but Adeline might well give him the cold shoulder after he failed to deliver on all the promises he had made her. Over and over the same question repeated itself in his mind: Where was Zeke?

Nathaniel hastened to The Chouteau House and learned, to his utter chagrin, that Ezekiel had not arrived.

The clerk nodded at several nearby maple chairs. "You're perfectly welcome to wait, if you like."

A rumble in Nathaniel's stomach reminded him that he had not eaten since morning. "Thank you, but I'll eat a meal and come back. By then he should be here."

"There's a tavern just around the corner called The Ark," the man recommended. "They serve fine hot meals."

"I don't know," Nathaniel said uncertainly.

"They have an excellent reputation, I can assure you."

"Why not?" Nathaniel said with a shrug. "I'll eat there and see you in an hour."

"If your uncle should show up, I'll inform him you've been here."

"Thank you," Nathaniel said, expressing his gratitude, and left. He found the tavern easily, and took a seat in the corner, then ordered a meal of chicken and corn bread. He hardly paid attention to the raucous drinkers, so concerned was he about his uncle, and consequently he experienced considerable surprise when a man abruptly took a seat at his table.

"Hello, there, good sir," the intruder said congenially, with just the slightest trace of a slur to his words, a broad smile on his oval face.

"Hello," Nathaniel automatically responded, the last forkful of chicken halfway to his lips. "May I help you?"

The man wore a fashionable black suit, a fur-collared cape, and an expensive beaver hat. Held in his left hand was a half-empty glass of whiskey. "I saw you sitting over here by yourself and thought you might be inclined to accept some companionship," he said.

"I'm not staying," Nathaniel said, and slid the fork into his mouth.

The other shrugged. "Well, no matter. I simply wanted to share a few drinks and conversation. Never let it be said that Joseph Lowe stays where he's not wanted," he declared and started to rise.

Aware he had unconsciously offended the stranger, and rating the man as a harmless drunk, Nathaniel set down his fork and said, "Hold on, Mr. Lowe. I don't mean to be stand-offish. I have a few minutes to share a drink with you."

Lowe beamed and faced around. "How kind of you. The drink will be on me. What are you having?"

"I could use another ale."

"Then ale it shall be," Lowe said, and bellowed for service. He gave the order and sat back in his chair. "I didn't catch your name?"

"King. Nathaniel King. My friends call me Nate."

"Pleased to meet you, Nate. I haven't seen you in here before, and I know most of the regulars."

"I'm new to St. Louis," Nathaniel divulged. "I've only been here a few days."

"And what do you think of our fair city?" Lowe inquired, and took a sip of whiskey.

"It's quite different from New York."

Lowe sat forward, all interest. "Is that where you're from, then? I've never been to New York City, but I've always wanted to see it. I was raised in Pittsburgh myself, but I haven't been home in many years."

"What do you do for a living, Mr. Lowe?"

"Call me Joe. I'm a speculator, Nate. Land, furs, trade

goods, you name it, I've dabbled in it at one time or another. What about yourself?''

"I was an accountant," Nathaniel said.

"Was?"

"Did I say was? I worked as an accountant in New York, and depending on how events develop here, I may be an accountant again after I return."

"Ahhhh. So you're planning to go back?"

"Yes. Hopefully within a few months. Everything depends on my uncle."

Lowe glanced around the tavern. "Your uncle? Is he here with you?"

"Not yet. I'm supposed to meet him at The Chouteau House later."

Lowe's eyebrows arched toward the smoke shrouded ceiling. "The Chouteau House? This uncle of yours must be rich."

"I don't know," Nathaniel replied. "I haven't seen him in ten years."

"He sent for you, did he?"

Nathaniel stared at the other man. "Why, yes. How did you know?"

"Simple logic. Here's to your uncle," Lowe said, and swallowed some more whiskey.

Nathaniel gazed at the front window, noticing the gathering twilight. "I should be leaving soon. My uncle might be there by now."

"I should be leaving too. Why don't I walk with you? The Chouteau House is on the way to the residence I'm renting."

"Fair enough," Nathaniel agreed, taking a shine to the friendly speculator. He paid his bill and followed Lowe out the door, then halted when the other man took a right. "Where are you going, Joe? The Chouteau House is this way," he said, pointing to the left.

"This is a shortcut. Your way we have to go around the corner and down the block. My way there is an alley that takes us almost to the entrance of The Chouteau House," Lowe stated.

Nathaniel hesitated, wondering if he could rely upon the other man, until Lowe gave him a friendly smile and hurried on. Chiding himself for being unduly suspicious, Nathaniel trailed after the speculator until they came to a narrow alley. He entered on Lowe's heels, passing a stack of crates propped against the right-hand wall. Three strides farther a hard object jammed him in the spine and a harder voice declared, "One word and you're a dead man."

# Chapter Five

As stark astonishment will eclipse reason, so instinct will eclipse both in a crisis, and such instinct has at times meant the difference between life and death for the person imperiled. Even as Nathaniel felt the object ram him in the back, an object he intuitively deduced to be a firearm and most likely a pistol, and even though he heard the gruff threat from his rear, he was about to react out of instinct and call out to his companion when Joseph Lowe did a most remarkable thing.

The alleged speculator suddenly whirled, a knife grasped in his right hand, and sneered at the youth. "You heard my friend, lad. Stand still or else."

Shock overcame whatever resistance Nathaniel might have offered, and he stood mute as Lowe pressed the knife against his abdomen and another man came around the left side holding a cocked pistol in his right hand.

"Let's see your money," Lowe directed.

"Money?" Nathaniel repeated, too dazed by the betrayal and abrupt turn of events to think clearly.

"Don't stall, boy!" Lowe snapped. "Your clothes hardly mark you as a pauper. You have a purse. I want it. Now."

Nathaniel sluggishly started to reach for his money in his inner pocket.

"Watch he doesn't pull on you!" warned the man with the gun, a weasel of a ruffian dressed in a gray coat and a green cap.

"This babe in the woods?" Lowe said contemptuously. "He won't resist."

The weasel snickered.

"In fact," Lowe went on, "I have half a mind to teach this lad a lesson he won't soon forget." He balled his left hand into a fist. "You should have stayed in New York, Nate. The East is a safe haven for pampered maggots like yourself. Out here only the strong survive."

Nathaniel's fingers closed on his money.

"Perhaps a broken nose will show you the error of your ways," Lowe stated, smirking.

At that juncture, as Lowe raised his fist to strike Nathaniel in the face, someone else spoke from the mouth of the alley, the words harsh and cracking like a whip. "And perhaps dying will teach you the error of yours."

Displaying lightning reflexes, the weasel pivoted toward the speaker, leveling his pistol as he turned, but as fast as he was, he wasn't fast enough. The thunderous boom of a large-caliber rifle was punctuated by the ball hitting the weasel in the right temple. The impact hurled the man from his feet to crash against the left-hand wall, where he collapsed in a heap, a neat hole marking the ball's entry point.

Lowe looked over Nathaniel's right shoulder, his eyes widening in alarm, and began to back away.

"Try me, cutthroat!" cried the newcomer in a resounding challenge, and the next moment a buckskin-clad figure rushed past Nathaniel, a gleaming hunting knife in his right hand.

Dumbfounded, his city-bred reflexes not equal to the occasion, Nathaniel could only gape as the two men closed. He caught a fleeting glimpse of his rescuer, a pantherish frontiersman attired in the typical garb of those who dwelt on the outskirts of civilization, and then the two men were feinting and thrusting, dodging and twisting, their blades weaving a glittering tapestry in the dusky air, the steel accenting the fading rays of the far-off setting sun that penetrated into the byways of the city.

Joseph Lowe fought with the ferocity of a cornered beast, but all his efforts were in vain. He tried every knife-fighting trick he knew, and each stab, each slash, was parried or evaded with bewildering ease.

Nathaniel saw the frontiersman press Lowe mercilessly, and then his rescuer, who wore a red cloth cap decorated with an odd length of swirling fur, sidestepped a frantic lunge and speared his knife into Lowe's chest.

Lowe stiffened and gasped, then stumbled backwards until he touched the wall, the hilt of the frontiersman's knife protruding from his ribs. He released his own knife and clutched at the hilt, but his limbs were too weak to extract the blade. His eyes wide, fear etched in his countenance, he gawked at his slayer. "You've killed me!" he cried.

"Take your medicine without whimpering, dog," the frontiersman said. "You've reaped your just desserts."

"Oh, God!" Lowe wailed, slipping downward slowly, blood trickling from the right corner of his mouth. "Oh, God!"

Both fascinated and horrified, Nathaniel watched the man die. He had hardly moved a muscle since entering the alley except to reach for his money, and now he realized his hand was still under his coat. He pulled it out and took a deep breath, dispelling the trance that held him. Hushed voices sounded to his rear and he glanced back, astounded to see over a dozen people.

"Help me!" Lowe whined. "Someone help me!"

The man in the buckskins walked over, took hold of his knife, and yanked it free, the blade dripping crimson over Lowe's clothes.

"No!" Lowe declared weakly, and made a sucking noise, as if he couldn't get enough air into his lungs.

Kneeling, the frontiersman looked Lowe in the eyes and started to wipe his knife clean on Lowe's coat. After a minute he stood and slid the hunting knife into a beaded sheath on his left hip.

Only then did Nathaniel gaze at his rescuer.

Like most mountain men and fur trappers who came from the distant plains and mountains to taste the sophisticated culture of St. Louis, this man radiated a raw vitality. His long brown hair, streaked with generous widths of gray, hung to below his shoulders. His blue eyes, as vivid as any mountain lake, regarded the world almost sternly, complementing his hawkish visage. From constant exposure to the sun and the elements, his skin had acquired a dark hue, nearly as dark as any Indian. His buckskins were beaded about the shoulders and down the seams. His moccasins were plain and worn. From the brown leather belt encircling his waist hung his knife and a bullet pouch.

"I want to thank you, sir, for saving my life," Nathaniel said.

A wry grin curled the mountain man's mouth, and he stared at Nathaniel with a curious expression, a mixture of relief and restrained mirth, before responding. "Do you now, Nate? That's nice to hear."

"How do you—" Nathaniel began, then focused on the red cap. A line from his uncle's letter rushed into his mind. "I'll be wearing the red so you know me." He impulsively stepped forward and placed his hands on the frontiersman's wide shoulders. "Ezekiel?"

The mountain man nodded and smiled. "Uncle Zeke to you."

Elated, Nathaniel felt himself taken in a bear hug and squeezed until he thought his back would break. He was abruptly released and inspected as if under a magnifying glass.

"By the Eternal, how you've grown!" Zeke declared heartily. "If that fellow at The Chouteau House hadn't given me a description, I'd never have known you."

"The desk clerk told you where to find me?"

Zeke nodded. "And you're fortunate I came straightaway instead of taking the time to unpack in my room." He glanced at the onlookers. "You let me handle this."

"Help me!' Lowe pleaded.

Nathaniel looked down at the robber, who was wheezing and moaning while more and more blood spurted from his mouth. Lowe returned the gaze with a pathetic, pleading countenance, silently imploring for aid beyond the power of any human agency to render.

"I'll put you out of your misery if you want," Zeke offered.

Lowe tried to focus on the frontiersman, but a fit of sputtering and coughing made him double over. He straightened, blubbered incoherently for several seconds, then suddenly stiffened and keeled over onto his right side, his blood-flecked mouth hanging open.

"Good riddance," Zeke said, and walked to the mouth of the alley. A large rifle was propped against the right-hand wall, and he scooped the gun into his arms and faced the growing crowd. "These men were attempting to rob my nephew," he announced, and pointed at the two corpses. "They were about to harm him when I arrived."

"Let me through! Let me through!" a man at the rear of the onlookers bellowed, and a moment later a portly gentleman dressed in a brown coat and breeches advanced to the forefront. His ruddy cheeks were accented by flared sideburns and prolific whiskers. He stared at the bodies in disapproval, then looked at the frontiersman.

Nathaniel tensed, anticipating trouble over the killings. In New York City, his uncle would be taken into custody and tossed into a jail until a trial could be convened. In St. Louis, where there was no police force, vigilante justice might prevail. To his surprise, the apparently distinguished citizen smiled and exclaimed happily, "Firebrand! Is it really you?"

"It's truly me, friend Osborne," Ezekiel responded.

"What brings you to these parts? We haven't seen you in, what, two years?"

"City life holds little attraction for a man who has learned to live in harmony with Nature," the frontiersman said solemnly.

"Ever the philosopher, eh?" Osborne replied good-naturedly, and glanced at Nathaniel. "Did I hear you say this is your nephew?"

"You did. Nathaniel King, my brother's son."

Osborne nodded. "I'm pleased to meet you, young man."

"My uncle did no wrong," Nathaniel said. "These ruffians were trying to take my money."

"So I gathered," Osborne responded. "Have no fear, Nathaniel. No one will hold these killings against your uncle. Those of us who have lived in St. Louis for a spell know your uncle well, and his word is widely respected."

"Osborne, I would be in your debt if you would see to it that these two scoundrels are disposed of properly," Zeke said.

"For you, Firebrand, anything," Osborne answered. "Will you be in town long?"

"No longer than necessary."

"Are you boarding in town?"

"The Chouteau House."

"Where else?" Osborne said, and chuckled. "I'll be around to visit you as soon as I can."

"We'll share a few drinks and talk over old times," Zeke proposed. He motioned for Nathaniel to come with him, and together they weaved through the crowd and departed.

"Where are you staying?" Zeke asked.

"The Bradley Hostelry," Nathaniel responded, staring at his uncle in awe, hardly able to believe they were reunited again.

"Let's fetch your belongings and move you in with me right away," Zeke said. "We have much to discuss."

"We certainly do," Nathaniel agreed, eager to keep the conversation going. He glanced at the length of grayish fur attached to the back of his uncle's cap. "Is that beaver fur?"

A burst of laughter erupted from the stout mountain man, and he shook his head vigorously. "I should say not, nephew. You have a lot to learn about the animals we'll encounter. Have you ever seen a beaver?"

"No," Nathaniel admitted.

"Have you ever laid eyes on a wolf?"

"No," Nathaniel replied again. "There are few wolves

left in New York. But I have seen paintings of wolves in books.''

"Then take a good look at my cap.''

Nathaniel complied, and after examining the fur for half a minute recognition dawned and he blurted out in amazement, ''It's a wolf tail!''

"Congratulations. Your lessons have begun.''

"But why would you wear a wolf tail on your head?''

"It's not that uncommon a practice," Zeke said. ''The *voyageurs* wear them quite often.''

"Who?''

"*Voyageurs*, nephew. Fur trappers. It's a French word.''

"Do you speak French?''

"A little. Out here it pays to learn as much as you can about everything.''

"But why a wolf tail?'' Nathaniel inquired out of curiosity, watching the unique adornment bob as his uncle walked.

"Because a mouse tail would look ridiculous," Zeke said with a grin.

Nathaniel had to laugh at the thought of a mouse tail on a hat. ''True.''

Ezekiel cradled his rifle in his arms and moved with a firm tread along the streets of the city, evidently knowing his way about, his sharp eyes constantly roving as he talked. ''There is a story behind this wolf tail. It belonged to old One Eye, the trickiest animal that ever lived. Some years back Shakespeare and I were trapping way up northwest of the Yellow Stone country. Something kept eating the beavers we caught along this one stream. In trap after trap we would find the beaver had been ripped to ribbons and partly devoured. This went on for a few weeks.'' He paused.

Enrapt in the story, Nathaniel hung on every word. His uncle possessed a natural flair for telling a tale, the consequences, most likely, of many an hour spent around a roaring campfire in the company of his friends. ''What did you do?''

"Shakespeare and I tried every ruse we knew to catch the culprit in the act, but nothing worked. We tried snares, double traps, even pits, but the beast helping itself to our catch was too crafty for us. We tried lying in hiding, but the animal always avoided us. Finally, we found a clear set of tracks at one of the kills and knew our nemesis was a wolf, which we had already conjectured. So we decided to dig a hole large enough for a man near one of the traps, and I went into the hole and waited."

"How long?"

"What? Oh, three days, I think."

"What did you eat? How did you survive?"

"I had a pouch of jerked meat with me," Zeke said, a twinkle in his eyes. "Anyway, on the third day this old wolf showed up. There was a beaver in the trap, so the wolf stalked close to it and pounced. Only then, when it was near the hole, did I see how big the beast was and discovered it had only one eye, the right. The left was as pale as the moon."

"And you shot him?"

"Not quite, nephew. I popped out of the hole, or tried to, but the dirt sides were too slippery and I fell on my face not two yards from old One Eye," Zeke related.

Nathaniel imagined how he would feel under such circumstances, and shuddered. "What happened then?"

Zeke looked at him. "What do you figure happened? Old One Eye was on me before I could move, his teeth bared, ready to tear me open."

"How did you kill it?" Nathaniel inquired, agog.

"I didn't. Old One Eye killed me," Zeke said, erupting in laughter and clapping his nephew on the shoulders.

They could have heard him all the way back in New York.

# Chapter Six

Seated in his uncle's plush room in The Chouteau House, Nathaniel gazed at the vibrant man he remembered so well from his childhood and shook his head in amazement, thinking he must be dreaming. Zeke's timely arrival had saved his money, if not his life, and in spite of the gulf of years and distance since last they had seen one another, he felt a warm bond with the older man. He gazed at the luxurious accommodations and inquired, "Why do you prefer to stay here? Isn't it expensive?"

Ezekiel surveyed the room disdainfully. "Civilization is difficult enough to abide as it is. Why suffer in a hovel when you can live first-class?"

The remark reminded Nathaniel of the treasure. "You must be quite wealthy."

"You think so?"

"You hinted as much in your letter."

"My letter?" Zeke repeated, his forehead furrowing. "Oh, you mean the greatest treasure in the world?"

Nathaniel leaned toward the upholstered chair in which his uncle sat a few feet away. "What kind of treasure is it, Uncle

Zeke? Have you made a fortune in the fur trade? Did you find gold? What?''

The frontiersman's lips seemed to tighten slightly. ''Is that what brought you out here, Nate? The treasure?''

''I won't lie to you. The treasure is part of the reason I came west, but I also wanted to see you again.''

''I see,'' Ezekiel said slowly, and slouched in his chair. ''You want to be rich, I gather?''

''I *need* to become rich.''

''Explain,'' Zeke directed.

So Nathaniel did, spending the better part of an hour relating his relationship with Adeline, his choice of a career as an accountant, and his marriage prospects without the wealth Adeline required.

Ezekiel King rarely interrupted, venturing a few questions now and then, listening to his favorite nephew with an air of sadness about him. Toward the end of Nathaniel's discourse, when Nate mentioned how much Adeline loved him, Zeke had to feign a sudden interest in his moccasins to conceal the scowl that automatically twisted his mouth.

''Now you understand the reason I must acquire the money necessary to support Adeline in the manner to which she is accustomed,'' Nathaniel mentioned.

''I understand perfectly.''

''Do you really intend to share your treasure with me?'' Nathaniel queried eagerly.

''I do.''

Overjoyed, Nathaniel beamed and glanced around the room. ''This is great news! By August I can be in New York again, proposing to Adeline.''

Zeke pursed his lips thoughtfully for a moment. ''Perhaps not.''

''What?''

''I didn't bring my treasure with me.''

Nathaniel was stunned. ''You didn't?''

''I couldn't,'' Zeke said.

''But you wrote in your letter that you would share it with me.''

"And I will, but to see my treasure you must return with me to my cabin in the Rocky Mountains."

The proposal shocked Nathaniel. He sank back in his chair, envisioning the dangers of a trek into the wild regions of the virtually unexplored Rocky Mountains. The risks were not his major concern. Rather, he was worried by the prospect of losing his life before he could return to civilization and his beloved Adeline.

"Does the idea bother you?" Ezekiel inquired.

"I was under the misimpression you were bringing your treasure to St. Louis," Nathaniel stated.

"I would if I could, nephew. But it would be impossible to transport such a treasure all the way from the Rockies to here."

"Couldn't you have brought a portion of it?"

"A portion would not be enough to satisfy you."

Nathaniel placed his elbows on his knees and rested his head in his hands. "I don't know what to do, Uncle Zeke. How long would such a trip take?"

"Months, at the very mimimum."

"How *many* months?"

"I doubt if you would be able to make it back here before winter sets in, so you would be obliged to wait until next spring. Ten months to a year, at least."

"A year?" Nathaniel exclaimed, and surged out of his chair. "I can't be away from Adeline for a year!"

"If she's truly the woman for you, she'll wait."

"But a *year!*" Nathaniel said, sitting down dejectedly.

Ezekiel sighed and stood. He crossed to a polished dresser and opened a drawer. "I'm sorry, Nate. I had no idea this would upset you so."

"I came so far," Nathaniel said softly.

"For which I'm grateful." Zeke removed a small leather pouch from the drawer and sat down again.

"My parents would be furious," Nathaniel predicted, and looked at his uncle. "Say, why haven't you asked any questions about Father or Mother or my brothers?"

"Your father and I parted ways years ago. Tell me. Does

he still refuse to talk about me to anyone?''

"Yes.''

Zeke shrugged. "There. You see? As far as your father and mother are concerned, I might as well be dead. And your older brothers and I were never as close as the two of us. You were always special to me, Nate. And to be quite honest, you're the only relative I give a damn about.''

"Since you're being honest, so will I,'' Nathaniel said. "If you share your treasure with me, I intend to share with them. They're my family, after all.''

"I would expect no less from you,'' Zeke said, and smiled. "Here. Take a gander at this.'' He flipped the small pouch into the air.

Nathaniel deftly caught the pouch and placed it in his lap. He loosened the drawstring and upended the contents into his left palm, his eyes widening when out tumbled seven golden nuggets, each the size of his thumbnail, each glittering in the light. "Are these what I think they are?''

Ezekiel nodded. "Gold. From the Rocky Mountains.''

"And you have more?''

"The Rocky Mountains are filled with gold. The Spaniards mined the region extensively years ago. I've come across several of their diggings and arrastra ruins in my travels.''

Nathaniel glanced up from the nuggets. "Why haven't there been any reports in the newspapers?''

"There will be,'' Zeke said, and gazed out the window at the lights of St. Louis. A melancholy settled upon him and he spoke in a low tone. "Eventually the word will become common knowledge. Now, only a few men such as myself are aware of the riches waiting to be plucked from the land to the west. I know a trapper who has a cabin situated near a creek where the bed is dotted with nuggets. You can walk along the bank and see them sparkle. But he hasn't touched them.''

Incredulous, Nathaniel straightened. "Why not?''

"Gold doesn't interest him.''

"Is he in his right mind?''

Ezekiel chuckled and nodded. "As sane as they come.

Gold is not the most valuable commodity in life, nephew.''

"It is to anyone with intelligence," Nathaniel said. "Look at yourself. You know how to use your gold wisely. You're staying at the best establishment in all of St. Louis."

A minute elasped before the frontiersman spoke, during which he regarded his nephew critically.

"Is something the matter?" Nathaniel inquired.

"Nothing that will not be remedied in due course."

Nathaniel began replacing the nuggets into the pouch. "How much time will I have to decide whether to go with you?"

"I'll need to know tomorrow."

A gleaming nugget almost dropped from Nathaniel's fingers. "Tomorrow? So soon? Surely you jest."

Zeke shook his head. "I leave for the mountains the day after tomorrow. You're welcome to come with me, if you like. If not, feel free to take those few nuggets with you to reimburse you for the expenses of your journey."

"But the treasure!"

"To see the treasure, you must see the Rockies."

"I'm at a loss to know what to do," Nathaniel confessed.

Ezekiel rose and moved to the window. He clasped his hands behind his broad back and contemplated the flurry of activity below: the carriages, carts, and wagons going to and fro, the individuals hastening home from work or en route to their favorite tavern or other night spot, and the many horses ridden by men from all walks of life. "I can sympathize with you, nephew. A decade ago I was in the same boat you are in."

"In what way, Uncle Zeke?"

"I had a similar decision to make. Whether to stay in New York or venture out west, whether to continue in the rut I was in or to take my life into my own hands and forge my own destiny."

"Why did you come out west?"

"Has your father told you much about my early life?" Zeke asked, still gazing at the street.

"No. Whenever I've tried to talk about you, he always

changed the subject.''

"How typical of Tom. He never could understand my reason for leaving. We argued for weeks before my departure and he accused me of abandoning the family, of losing my proper perspective. I'm five years older than your father, and yet he had the gall to say I was acting like a ten-year-old.''

Nathaniel relaxed in the chair, listening attentively, intensely curious about his uncle's past. "You weren't married, were you?"

"No," Ezekiel said. "I almost married once, when I was twenty. Rebecca was her name, and she was the loveliest woman I ever laid eyes on. We courted and made plans to raise our own children. I was in business with Tom at the time, helping him launch the construction business." He paused, his shoulders slumping. "And then my world fell apart. Rebecca died."

"What happened?"

"Consumption. Can you believe it? A healthy young woman like her and she died from consumption."

"Consumption can strike anyone at any age," Nathaniel noted, then felt awkward over having made such a trite observation.

Ezekiel did not speak for a while, and when he did he seemed to be talking from a great distance, not literally but emotionally. "Rebecca's death crushed me. For years I drifted through life, going through the motions without bothering about the meaning of anything I did. I worked hard, putting in long hours, only because I had nothing else to do. Try as I might, I could not bring myself to court another woman. Rebecca was the only woman I've ever loved."

Nathaniel said nothing.

"I had often considered the notion of leaving New York, of heading for the frontier. I wanted to view the wonders of the unexplored lands for myself, but I kept concocting excuses for why I shouldn't go. When I'd bring the subject up to Tom, he'd always ridicule it as juvenile thinking." Zeke sighed. "I lost count of how many hours I spent reading about

Lewis and Clark and other explorers. I would often spend my days off in the woods, and I fancied myself as a bit of an outdoorsman.''

"And one day you just up and took off?''

"Yes. One day I cut out for the frontier. I had saved a fair sum of money with which to outfit myself, and I joined a group of settlers who were heading westward. This was in 1818, and we arrived in Missouri about the same time the territory was admitted to the Union. The fur trade is the state's most important industry, and I naturally became a trapper for the American Fur Company. That's how I met Shakespeare."

"You mentioned him earlier. Who is he?''

"My best friend in all the world. Shakespeare McNair.''

"What a strange name.''

Ezekiel laughed. "Many of the men who live on the frontier have acquired unusual sobriquets. Shakespeare got his because he likes to quote Shakespeare all the time.''

"You wrote home once, didn't you?''

"Yes, about nine years ago. I told Tom about my employment with the American Fur Company and praised the new lands I had seen. I never received an answer.''

"I think Father tossed your letter out.''

"That would be Tom,'' Zeke said sadly. "Oh, well. He always was a stubborn cuss.''

"What happened next?''

"I trapped for the American Fur Company for two years, and then Shakespeare and I decided to become free trappers. We headed for the Rocky Mountains, and except for occasional treks to St. Louis and elsewhere, that's where I've made my home.''

"Did you ever have the desire to visit New York?''

The frontiersman turned. "Never.''

Nathaniel performed some mental calculations. "Only ten of your forty-eight years have been spent on the frontier, and yet you seem at home in the wilds.''

Zeke's eyes bored into his nephew's. "Out here, Nate, either you adjust and adapt or you die. It's as simple as that.''

"That man Osborne, where do you know him from?"

"I met him on the way to Missouri. We've been friends ever since."     •

"Why did he call you Firebrand?"

Ezekiel chuckled. "Think nothing of it. Firebrand is a nickname Osborne bestowed upon me when we had a slight misunderstanding with a band of Indians who refused to allow our wagons to pass through their territory unless we gave them two thirds of our horses and twelve rifles."

"What happened?"

A cloud seemed to descend over Ezekiel's countenance. "The red rascals didn't get one horse or rifle."

Nathaniel decided to ask Osborne for the particulars if ever the opportunity presented itself. "Here, Uncle," he said, and returned the pouch of gold nuggets.

"I'll be turning in early," Zeke announced. "I traveled long and hard to reach St. Louis today, and after that fracas in the alley I'm a mite tuckered out."

"Do you mind if I stay up for a while? I have a lot to think about," Nathaniel commented.

"Stay awake as long as you like, Nate," Zeke said, depositing the pouch in the dresser drawer. "You have the most important decision of your life to make."

"If I decide to stay, I'll have to write my family and Adeline and explain the situation."

"Go right ahead," Zeke responded, moving to the side of the bed. He noticed a book lying beside his nephew's open bags, which they had placed on the bed when they first arrived. "What's this?" he asked, and scooped the book into his right hand.

"*The Last of the Mohicans.*"

"James Fenimore Cooper," Zeke said thoughtfully. "I've heard of him. Isn't he the one who writes about Leatherskin?"

"That's Leatherstocking, Uncle Zeke."

"Whatever. Some of my friends have read his other books. They say he writes well."

"You're welcome to read it if you wish."

"Thanks. Perhaps I will. It has been a while since I've

read anything, and in New York I read all the time.'' Zeke wagged the book in his hand. ''Oh, well. Reading always was a substitute for experience.''

Nathaniel watched his uncle prepare the bed. He envisioned his darling Adeline, far, far away in New York, and he closed his eyes. A single question repeated itself over and over in his mind: *What am I going to do?*

# Chapter Seven

What choice did he have?

If he wanted to please Adeline—and pleasing her was more important to him than breathing—he had to accumulate the fortune he would need to support her lavish style of life. He considered returning to New York City and going to work for her father, but the prospect of spending years in the mercantile profession did not appeal to him, especially as every moment would be spent under the watchful eyes of her stern father. If wealthy he must be, then he would acquire the wealth by his own initiative and not be dependent on another man for his livelihood. For the sake of Adeline, he convinced himself, he must make the journey to the Rocky Mountains and obtain his share of Ezekiel's treasure.

But there was another reason, a reason he scarcely admitted, although at the back of his mind he realized the truth. The idea of heading farther west, into the rugged, unmapped regions of the unknown, appealed to his adventurous spirit. He had supreme confidence in his Uncle Zeke, and believed that Ezekiel would see him safely through any ordeal. In addition, he kept thinking about the adventures of Leatherstocking, and he wondered if he just might, perhaps, have an adventure or two of his own before he saw St. Louis again.

Few men can resist the siren song of love and the dictates of the heart. Even fewer can resist the overpowering drives of human nature. So it was that with a clear conscience and a happy, expectant soul Nathaniel informed his uncle of his decision at first light the next morning. "I've decided to go with you."

Ezekiel bounded out of bed and pranced around like a panther dancing a jig, clapping his hands and cackling as if at a great triumph. After a couple of minutes he halted abruptly and beamed down at Nathaniel. "Nephew, you will never regret your decision. This I can promise you."

"I'll believe that when I see the light in Adeline's eyes as I show her my gold."

Zeke straightened, suddenly sober. "Of course. The gold. Well, we should have breakfast and commence outfitting you for the trip."

"I can buy my own supplies," Nathaniel offered.

"Nonsense. Since this was my idea, and since I'm the one with the gold nuggets, I insist on paying for your gear and clothes."

"Clothes? What's wrong with the clothes I already own?"

Zeke laughed and glanced at the apparel in question, draped over the back of a nearby chair. "Those clothes are all right for city life, even for travel east of the Mississippi, but you'll need far better if you want to be comfortable beyond the frontier."

"But I paid good money for them in New York," Nathaniel persisted.

"New York clothes are mainly for dandies and squires who don't know beans about life outdoors. Trust me," Zeke said.

"I trust you," Nathaniel replied, still not entirely convinced of his need for new clothing.

Ezekiel noticed and placed his hands on his hips. "What are your trousers made of?"

"Wool."

"And your coat?"

"Wool."

"And your hat?"

"Wool. But what does that matter?"

"If the Eternal had meant for man to wear wool, He would have made us sheep," Zeke stated. "Wool is fine for city uses or on a farm, but out west, where you'll be subjected to the worst weather Nature can throw at you, where you can start out hot at the base of a mountain and be in ten feet of snow by the time you reach the summit, you want buckskins. Wool can shrink, nephew. Wool falls to pieces after a month or two of mountain living. Buckskins do not."

"Are you saying I need buckskins?" Nathaniel inquired, secretly pleased by the idea.

"Buckskins and much more."

"Then I guess I'm in your hands."

"Have you ever fired a gun?"

The unexpected question gave Nathaniel pause. He almost lied, but changed his mind. "No."

"Not *ever*?"

"Never."

Ezekiel shook his head and clucked. "What has my brother done to you?"

"Don't blame my father. Why should I have fired a gun when there are no hostile Indians in New York and all the food we ate could be bought at the market or the butcher?"

"I can see your point, but it's still a tragedy when a boy has grown to manhood and hasn't learned to fire a rifle. How is a youngster to learn the qualities of self-reliance and independence if he doesn't know how to feed and clothe himself? If this is what cities do to our youth, then they are more vile than I imagined. Cities breed slaves to civilization, nephew, and produce men and women who are in bondage to the mercantile and the slaughterhouse."

"I never gave the matter much thought."

"I have. Did you know your father and I hunted quite avidly when we were young?"

Nathaniel's surprise showed. "No, I didn't. We don't even have a gun in the house now. He won't allow them."

"Probably because they remind him of me," Zeke speculated. He walked to the south wall, where he had propped his rifle, and held the gun out. "Do you know what this is, Nate?"

"A rifle."

"More than a rifle, nephew. It's a Hawken. The best damn gun ever made, and they're made right here in St. Louis by Jacob and Samuel Hawken, friends of mine. Mine is a .60-caliber, and I've knocked down a buffalo at two hundred yards with it."

"Two hundred yards?" Nathaniel repeated skeptically.

"One day maybe you'll do even better."

"Will you teach me to shoot yours?"

"No. I'll teach you to shoot yours."

Nathaniel came out of the bed so fast he stubbed his right foot on the night table. "You'll buy me a rifle of my very own?"

"That's the general idea, nephew. We'd be in a sorry state if two grizzlies decided that we were their tasty supper and we only had one rifle between us."

"My own rifle," Nathaniel said softly, thrilled.

Ezekiel smiled and nodded at his nephew's clothes. "Get your britches on, Nate. We have a lot to do today if we hope to leave this serpent's den tomorrow."

Nathaniel would always remember that day as long as he lived, the first of many memorable days he would experience in the months ahead. He followed his uncle from establishment to establishment like an eager young puppy anxious to please its new master, listening to tales about Zeke's years on the frontier, tales that prompted him, more than once, to gaze at the western horizon with longing in his eyes.

Ezekiel went on a buying spree, not only for the equipment and supplies his nephew would need, but for provisions he required to restock the depleted stores at his remote cabin. He paid for most of the items with cash or coin, although on two occasions, when he bought buckskins for Nathaniel and when he purchased three pistols, two for the youth and one for himself, he paid with a few of his gold nuggets.

The buckskins were obtained at a store named Farber's, where the owner, a former trapper himself, specialized in goods for those engaged in the fur trade. One of his employees was quite skilled at constructing custom-made garments from the many skins and furs the owner received in barter. Upon learning, however, that the employee had more work than he could handle and that buckskins for Nathaniel would take four days to be stitched together, Zeke became annoyed at the prospect of staying in St. Louis beyond his alloted departure date. The owner came to their rescue by suggesting Nathaniel try on one of the dozen or so sets of buckskins that had never been claimed by their purchasers and were gathering dust on a shelf at the back of the store.

To Nathaniel's delight, he found buckskins that fit him, although rather loosely. Once he donned the soft, pliable deerskin garments, including a pair of moccasins that rose almost to his knees, he felt as if he were a new man. He ran his fingers over the dressed deerskin again and again, thinking he should pinch himself to see if he was dreaming.

Ezekiel studied his nephew for a minute, then commented, "Not a bad fit. We'll make you another set after we reach my cabin."

"I don't know if I can thank you enough."

"Shucks, Nate. We're just getting started."

Next Nathaniel acquired a wide leather belt to which he attached a hunting knife sporting a 12-inch blade in a plain sheath. His uncle helped him select a powder horn, which he hung over his left shoulder by means of a thin strap, angling it across his chest to ride high on his right hip, within easy reach. He also obtained a large pouch for his bullets, bullet mould, ball screw, wiper, and awl. As he was adjusting the bullet pouch under the powder horn, his uncle approached bearing a red and black Mackinaw coat.

"Try this on for size," Zeke said.

"A red coat?" Nathaniel responded.

"What's wrong with it?"

"Won't Indians and game be able to spot me too easily?"

"Beaver, bear, and deer don't care if you're wearing red, blue, or purple. With a Hawken in your hands, it doesn't matter if the game spots you or not."

"But what about the Indians?"

"I've been wearing a red cap for years and I still have my scalp," Zeke said, then surreptitiously winked at Eugene Farber, who stood nearby. "But if it worries you, just remember the best method for getting out of Indian trouble. It never fails."

"What is it?"

"Run like hell."

After trying on the Mackinaw coat, which fit perfectly, Nathaniel added the garment to his growing collection. His uncle continued to buy provisions, some of which they were to pick up the next day on their way out of St. Louis. There were spare flints and locks, 200 pounds of lead, 60 pounds of powder, a few spare knives, two pipes and tobacco, and much more.

From Farber's they went to a small shop where Ezekiel bought the three pistols. He stuck two of them under his nephew's belt, stood back, studied the pistols and the knife, and nodded. "You look green, but I can guarantee no one will try to rob you now."

Their last visit of the day was to the Hawken brothers, Jacob and Samuel, who were kept busy meeting the great demand for their superb rifles. Both men were soft-spoken and dedicated to their craft. They greeted Ezekiel warmly and listened to his request for a rifle for Nathaniel.

"What caliber would you prefer?" Samuel inquired, scrutinizing Nathaniel closely. "Since it's his first plains rifle, I would recommend a .40-caliber."

"If a man is going to carry a rifle, he should carry one that will stop any brute or hostile he meets," Zeke declared. "Give Nate a .60-caliber."

The Hawken brothers glanced at one another, and Jacob shrugged and said, "As you wish. Would you care for us to instruct him in its use?"

"Go right ahead."

Into Nathaniel's tingling hands was delivered a heavy .60-caliber Hawken. He hefted the rifle, admiring the smooth 34-inch octagonal barrel, the sturdy stock with its cresent-shaped butt plate, the low sights, and the percussion lock.

Samuel Hawken smiled. "This rifle will serve you in good stead, young man. But you must always remember that a rifle is only as good as the man who uses it. A rifle is a tool, nothing more. Keep it clean and protect it from the elements, and you may find that it rewards you by saving your life."

"I'll take good care of it," Nathaniel promised.

Samuel nodded knowingly. "I expect you will. I can recall how I felt about my first rifle. Now allow me to show you how to load and fire it."

For 20 minutes Nathaniel was instructed in the proper use of a plains rifle by the two brothers, who seemed to derive considerable enjoyment from the teaching. They showed him how to load the ball, how to use the ramrod properly, and gave him tips on priming. They advised him that there would be a slight kick to the .60-caliber, a negligible recoil that would not hamper a fast reload in an emergency. Nathaniel thanked them for their kindness and walked out the front door feeling strangely euphoric.

"We'll need to find a cover for your rifle," Zeke mentioned as they headed for The Chouteau House. "You'll want to keep it dry and handy at all times once we're on the prairie."

Staring at his new gun, his forehead creased as he remembered the duel between Tyler and Clancy, Nathaniel voiced a question. "Have you killed a *lot* of men, Uncle Zeke?"

"Killing is part and parcel of frontier life. You might never need to kill a white man, but as sure as the sun rises and sets every day you'll have to kill an Indian or two," the frontiersman said. "And yes, I've killed my fair share. Why?"

"Oh, nothing."

"Don't you think you could shoot another human being?"

"I don't know."

"When the time comes to do it, you'll do it."

Nathaniel glanced at his uncle. "How can you be so certain?"

"Because when the time comes, it will either be you or the other fellow, whether white or Indian. And when someone is about to knife you, or scalp you, or put a ball in your head, you'll find that the Good Lord put a sense of self-preservation in us for a reason. Only a fool or a weakling rolls over and dies without giving a good account of himself. On the frontier and in the unexplored regions it's often kill or be killed.''

''I don't want to die,'' Nathaniel said softly.

''Who does?''

# Chapter Eight

Ezekiel and Nathaniel King rode out of St. Louis on the morning of May 6 under a sunny sky and with a light breeze from the northwest to cool their faces. Nathaniel rode his mare, Zeke a roan gelding, and both led pack horses loaded with their provisions. They followed the winding course of the Missouri River along a well-used dirt road. The state of Missouri had been admitted to the Union in 1821 as a slave state, and there were already 70,000 people living in the westernmost frontier of the nation.

Nathaniel soaked up the sights and sounds with a keen relish. They were not in any danger from the Indians in Missouri, who had signed a peace treaty with the U.S. government some years back, so he could relax and enjoy the trip. He noticed that his uncle seemed to be in a hurry; they only spent two hours in Independence. Eight days after they left St. Louis they came to the farthest outpost of civilization, Westport Landing, near the point where the Missouri and Kansas Rivers met. The trading post there, founded by a Frenchman in 1821, did a bustling business with trappers, hunters, and Indians, and served as a stopping-

off point for the traders from Missouri en route to Santa Fe
to do business with the Spanish.

Two hours after they arrived, an incident occurred that
Nathaniel would have reason to reflect on later. His uncle
had selected a campsite to the southeast of the trading post,
and they were busily engaged in bedding down for the
night, when Nathaniel saw his uncle straighten and stare
intently at three men who were riding toward the post.
Puzzled, he looked at the riders, all three of whom were
hulking, unkempt types attired in shabby buckskins. None
of the men so much as glanced in their direction. He shrugged
and went back to unfolding a blanket.

At first light they were packed and off, heading west across
the rolling prairie, staying close to the Kansas River. In front
of them stretched more than two million square miles of
pristine wilderness.

Nathaniel cradled his rifle in the crook of his right arm
and admired the scenery. Low grass covered the ground for
as far as the eye could see, interspersed with colorful,
beautiful flowers. Now and then they would come across a
small brook that intersected the river. Cedar trees and others
grew along the banks. Occasionally a large fish would leap
out of the water and splash down again.

At midday Ezekiel called a halt. He dismounted and stood
staring along their back trail for several minutes.

"Is something wrong?" Nathaniel asked.

Zeke frowned. "I'm the biggest fool who ever lived."

"I don't understand."

"By the Eternal, I should have known better!" Zeke
snapped angrily.

Nathaniel gazed eastward and saw nothing but the
picturesque expanse of prairie. "Known better about what?"

"About paying for the pistols and the buckskins with
gold."

"Why?"

"Because gold loosens lips. Folks start to talk. And then
the wrong people hear about it."

"Like robbers?"

"And worse," Ezekiel said, and sighed. "We're being followed, nephew."

Nathaniel looked eastward again. "I don't see anyone."

"Keep watching."

Squinting in the warm sunlight, Nathaniel fixed his eyes on the eastern horizon. To his surprise, barely perceptible figures materialized in the distance, and he guessed they were three men on horseback. "I see three riders."

Zeke nodded. "The same ones who were at Westport Landing, no doubt."

"They've trailed us all the way from St. Louis?"

"I reckon they have."

"If they want your nuggets, why didn't they jump us sooner?"

"They're hoping we'll lead them to where I found the gold," Zeke said. "They'll trail us all the way to the Rocky Mountains if I let them."

"How can we stop them?"

Ezekiel vented a harsh laugh. "There are all sorts of ways, nephew."

"Should we keep going then?"

"No. We'll take a break and rest the horses. We don't want the varmints to know we're on to them."

Nathaniel had lost much of his appetite. He kept glancing at the eastern horizon, hoping his uncle was mistaken, and wondering how he would fare when the confrontation came. Since leaving New York he had seen three men die, and the future, as Zeke had indicated, promised to hold more death in store for him. But could he squeeze the trigger when the time came? His uncle believed he could, but Ezekiel had spent a decade living as a savage lived. For Zeke killing must be easy.

"You have nothing to be nervous about yet, Nate," Zeke commented.

"Will they try to kill us?"

"Not until they're convinced I won't lead them to the gold. They're fools, in addition to being worthless vermin. They probably make a living by robbing other trappers and traders.''

"What will you do to them?"

"Wait and see."

In 20 minutes they were mounted and resuming their journey. To take his mind off the men shadowing them, Nathaniel concentrated on the wildlife they encountered and asked his uncle about each species, learning the habits of all the game on the plains. They saw deer and antelope in abundance, and several days later spied the first of many elk. There were birds and hawks, eagles and owls. But Nathaniel had yet to spy the animal he most wanted to see.

"Uncle Zeke, where are all the buffalo?" he inquired when they turned up the Republican Fork of the Kansas River.

"We're not quite to buffalo country yet," Ezekiel answered. "They don't quite range this far east, although I was told by a Caw chief that they did graze in this vicinity many years ago."

"Why haven't we seen any Indians yet either? I was under the impression they are all over these plains."

"They are. A small band was watching us about three hours ago."

Nathaniel stiffened in the saddle. "They were?"

"Calm down, nephew. Not all Indians are hostile. The main ones to worry about are the Blackfeet, the Arikara, the Sioux, and the Cheyenne. That's just on the plains. If you ever head to the Old Southwest, down Santa Fe way, you'll have to guard your scalp against the Comanches, Kiowas, and the Apaches."

"Have you fought many Indians, Uncle Zeke?"

"More than I care to remember."

"How do you feel about them?"

"Feel about them?"

"Yes. Do you hate the Indians?"

Ezekiel glanced at his kin. "Now why would I hate them?"

"There have been a lot of stories in the press back east about what to do with the Indians. Some folks think we should let them live on their lands in peace. Others, those who seem to despise the Indians, want to force them out of the way by having the government relocate them," Nathaniel mentioned. "Andrew Jackson, who's running for President again, says the Indians are an inferior race and that we have an obligation to reorganize them according to our way of doing things."

"Jackson said that, did he?"

"Yes. I read about it in the paper. A lot of people agree with him."

Ezekiel gazed westward and sighed. "I know about Old Hickory, Nate. Why do you think he acquired a nickname like that? Because he's an unyielding bastard who can not abide another point of view than his own. He always believes he's right and the rest of the world is wrong. Mark my words. If that pompous ass is elected, there will be hell to pay with the Indians."

Nathaniel pondered those words as they rode onward. Five days later he encountered his first tribe when they rode to the sloping crest of a low hill and there, encamped near the Republican river, were dozens of Indians.

"Otos," Zeke declared.

"Are they friendly?"

"As friendly as they come."

Reassured but still anxious, Nathaniel retained a firm grip on his rifle as he followed his uncle down to the Indian camp. He saw that the tribe lived in pole huts covered with straw and dirt. The women hung back while the men advanced to meet Zeke and him. There were few guns in evidence, and most of the men wore little more than a buckskin loincloth, if that. They impressed him as being a poor clan, not one of the great warlike plains tribes he had heard so much about.

A stocky Indian stepped in front of the rest and moved his hands and arms in a peculiar series of gestures.

Nathaniel was about to inquire as to the meaning when his uncle responded with a similar sequence. Perplexed, he surveyed the Otos, relieved to see none of them displayed the slightest hostility.

Ezekiel dismounted and walked to his pack horse. He extracted a hunting knife and presented it to the stocky Indian. After a few more hand gestures he climbed aboard his stallion, smiled and nodded, and rode through the clan.

Amused, Nathaniel observed the stocky Indian proudly displaying the hunting knife. He stayed on his uncle's heels and didn't speak until they had passed the village. "What was that all about, Uncle Zeke?"

"Their chief wanted us to smoke with them."

"Smoke?"

"Smoke a pipe, nephew. Do you know how to smoke?"

"No."

"Then you'd best learn. Every Indian tribe I know has a smoking ceremony. When an Indian offers to smoke with you, it means he has no intention of doing you harm. The ceremony is supposed to mean that your hearts and minds are one."

"Why didn't you smoke with him?"

"Because of those sons of bitches after us. I told him there were bad white men on our trail and we couldn't afford to stop. To show I was sincere and not offering an insult, I gave him that knife."

"You talked to him with your hands?" Nathaniel inquired in amazement.

Zeke nodded. "They call it sign language. Every Indian uses it. Learn sigh language and you can parley with any tribe on the plains, no matter what language they may speak."

"Who taught sign language to you?"

"Shakespeare. And I'll teach you. By the time we reach my cabin, you'll be an old hand at it."

"How long will it take us to reach your cabin, anyway?"

"If we're lucky, about four weeks. Maybe a bit less. We'll follow the Republican to within seventy-five miles or so of the Rockies. Then we have quite a haul up to the high country. We could shave time by cutting straight across instead of sticking with the river, but there's more game this way," Zeke explained, and smiled. "And I wouldn't want you to starve to death before you see the treasure."

"I can hardly wait," Nathaniel admitted.

"We won't be spending much time at the cabin when we get there," Zeke remarked.

The statement surprised Nathaniel. "Why not?"

"Because if we don't run into any problems, if we don't get sick or snake-bit or scalped, I want to push on to the rendezvous."

"The what?"

Ezekiel stared at his young nephew and shook his head. "It's hard to believe I was as green as you once. The rendezvous is held each summer. Practically everybody involved in the fur trade shows up for a month or so of the wildest goings-on you'll ever see. This year the rendezvous is to be held at Bear Lake, up in the same neck of the woods as the Great Salt Lake."

"I read about the Great Salt Lake in the papers."

"You sure must read those newspapers a lot."

"Why shouldn't I?"

"Newspapers are like a gabby gossip. They're just so much hot air."

In another mile they came to a stand of thick cedar and pine trees. Zeke took a faint trail running along the bank of the river, and when they passed the trees he suddenly wheeled his mount. "This will do," he announced.

"Are we making camp already?"

"No," Zeke said, and rode into the thickest part of the stand. He dropped to the ground and secured the reins to a firm limb.

Nathaniel followed suit, wondering what his uncle could be up to now. He tied his horses, then walked with Zeke to the Republican.

"Water, nephew, is the key to survival in the wilderness. Learn to sniff out water and you'll never need to worry about thirst or starvation. Every living beast needs water to survive. Deer, elk, buffalo. Find the water and you find them," Ezekiel stated, and stared at the surrounding plains with admiration reflected in his eyes. "Some folks happen to think that game is scarce in these parts, but it isn't unless you're with a big party that scares every living critter within miles into hiding. The Otos and the Caws make a living hereabouts, and so can a white man if he learns their secret. The Indians learned to live the natural way ages ago, and they have a lot to teach us if we'll just give a listen."

"Are we going to fish here?" Nathaniel inquired, watching the sluggush flow of water.

"No." Ezekiel faced east. "I asked the Oto chief to delay those three varmints trailing us as long as he could. If they smoke with him, they'll be hell-bent for leather to catch up with us. They'll come along our back trail as fast as they can, and they won't be as cautious as they might be otherwise."

"If the Otos are going to delay them, shouldn't we be making tracks? Maybe we can lose them."

"We're not going anywhere, Nate," Zeke said slowly, and motioned at the trees. "We'll wait right here until those snakes-in-the-grass show their ugly faces, and then we'll put all that target-shooting you've been doing every time we stop to good use." He grinned. "We'll kill them."

# Chapter Nine

"We can't just kill them, Uncle."

"Watch me," Zeke said, walking into the trees.

"But we don't really know that they're after us," Nathaniel said, staying one step behind. "They could be on their way to the Rocky Mountains, same as us."

"They're not."

Nathaniel took hold of his uncle's right arm and swung Zeke around. "You don't *know* that!"

"I know it," Zeke maintained obstinately.

"I can't believe you would murder someone in cold blood."

"Better I do unto them before they do unto me."

His anger mounting, Nathaniel glanced eastward, relieved the trio weren't in sight, then tore into his uncle again. "How do you plan to kill them? Shoot them from ambush?"

"I'll ask them to turn around and smile before I squeeze the trigger," Zeke said sarcastically. He frowned and studied the younger man for a minute, noting the set of Nate's jaw and the fire in his nephew's eyes.

"If you do this," Nathaniel warned, "I'll return to St. Louis."

"All by yourself?"

"With or without your assistance."

Ezekiel rested the barrel of his Hawken on his right shoulder. "You'd go back without seeing the treasure?"

Nathaniel nodded.

"Then this must mean more to you than I figured," Zeke said. "How would you feel if I can prove those men aim to kill us or rob us?"

"I'd stand by your side come what may."

"Fair enough," Zeke said, and scrutinized the lay of the land. He pointed at two cedar trees growing close to one another 30 feet to the south. "Those trees should do you."

"For what?"

"As a shield. Hunker down in the grass behind those trees and wait until they go for their guns."

Nathaniel glanced at the trees. "What do you have in mind?"

"You don't trust me, Nate, and that cuts me to the quick. If you won't accept my leadership now, what are you going to do later, when we run into unfriendly Indians or some other danger? I can't afford to argue with you every time there's killing to be done. Out here, killing is just part of staying alive."

"You still haven't told your plan."

"It's simple. You'll wait behind those trees and I'll wait by the river. When those three upstanding citizens catch up with us, we'll play it by ear. If they're friendly, as you claim, then we won't raise a hand against them. But if they're not, if they try to kill me, I'll be counting on you to back my play."

"Shoot them?"

"You can club them to death for all I care. Just don't let them do me in."

Nathaniel licked his lips, nervousness seizing him, and fidgeted. "I don't know if I can," he confessed.

"Now is a hell of a time to turn Quaker on me."

"I've never shot anyone before."

"I know. You told me, remember? Well, nephew, as the saying goes, there's a first time for everything," Zeke said, and chuckled. He strolled toward the bank. "Now remember, if one of those rascals takes a bead on me, you can pretty much take it for granted he doesn't have peaceful intentions."

"Uncle Zeke, let's keep riding," Nathaniel urged.

"Another rule to remember is this, nephew. If you can't avoid a fight, then be damn sure you get in the first lick. A word to the wise," Zeke stated. He reached the bank and squatted down, facing to the east.

Stunned at the likelihood of imminent violence, Nathaniel shuffled to the cedar trees and knelt in the soft grass to their rear. He fingered the Hawken and gulped. Despite the seasoned reasoning of his uncle, he couldn't shake a gnawing, growing feeling of outright fear. Not fear for his personal safety, but fear over the inner consequences of slaying a fellow human being. He knew he wasn't the most devoutly religious person on the continent, but his parents had raised him to attend church every week and to respect the Ten Commandments. And one of those commandments was as plain as the nose on his face: Thou shalt not kill.

Not ever.

So what would happen to his soul if he slew one of the three men, even if they were robbers or killers? What were the eternal consequences of violating the commandment not to take a life? His uncle had taken the lives of two men back in St. Louis and had hardly given the matter a second thought. And Tyler, the gambler, had been all too ready to take Clancy's life on the field of honor. But they were grown men. They'd already made their peace with the world, or at least they had rated their priorities and adhered to their own personal code of conduct.

But what about me? Nathaniel asked himself. He would be 20 in November. By Eastern standards he was already a man. By the values practiced on the frontier he was still a green kid, wet behind the ears. He'd already taken the first step toward manhood by asserting his independence. Over what mysterious threshold would killing another man take him? Did he automatically become a man by the standards of the West if he participated in bloodshed? Jim Bowie was widely considered to be a brave man, and yet what was he

most noted for? Killing with his famous knife. Andrew
Jackson had acquired a reputation as a fearless man. And
how? By killing Creek and Seminole Indians in the South,
and by killing the British at New Orleans. Killing one's
enemies, it seemed, constituted a badge of courage in the
eyes of most men.

But was it *right*?

Nathaniel touched his pistols, working them up and down
under his belt to ensure they were loose and ready to be used.
His mouth felt extremely dry and he craved a sip of water.

"Here they come!" Ezekiel suddenly called out.

Startled, Nathaniel glanced to the east. Through the trees
he glimpsed them in the distance, riding hard, approaching
rapidly. Even at that range he recognized them as the same
three hulking riders he had seen at Westport Landing, and
a chill rippled down his spine. He promptly drew his pistols
and placed them to his right, then flattened and extended the
Hawken between the cedar trees.

Ezekiel stood and cradled his rifle across his waist. He
watched the trio draw ever nearer, his visage calm, his hands
steady.

How does he do it? Nathaniel marveled, and placed his
right thumb on the hammer, his finger already lightly
caressing the trigger. He heard the sound of hooves
drumming on the hard earth, and the sound grew louder and
louder. Then the cadence abruptly slackened off.

The three riders had spotted Ezekiel. They immediately
slowed to a walk, less than 100 yards from the stand of trees,
and began conversing animatedly.

Nathaniel pressed the Hawken to his shoulder and glued
his eyes to the three scruffy men, breathing shallowly, his
pulse quickening.

After a brief discussion the trio advanced in a line with
the largest man in the middle. All three carried rifles and
had pistols stuck in their belts. All three appeared capable
of giving a baby nightmares.

Please let them be peaceful! Nathaniel thought, his
abdomen tightening into a knot. When they were 20 yards
from his uncle, so close that he could see the nostrils of the

large man's horse flare, he cocked his rifle.

Displaying an attitude of complete unconcern, Ezekiel smiled and gave a little wave with his left hand. "Howdy, strangers!" he hailed them. "Am I pleased to see you."

Nathaniel saw the three men exchange glances, and the one on the right grinned slyly for a few seconds until he realized what he was doing and sobered. The grin was a bad omen. Nathaniel's instincts told him that his uncle had been right, that the trio were up to no good, and he realized there would be violence without a doubt. The certainty shook him.

"Hello, friend," the large rider declared when the trio was 40 feet from Ezekiel. They approached to within two yards before stopping. All three were glancing every which way, as if they suspected a trap. "This is a bad land in which to be afoot."

"You've hit the nail on the head there, stranger," Ezekiel agreed, just as friendly as a minister.

"Where's your horse?"

"Wouldn't you know it?" Zeke said and laughed. "My horse and my pack animal both lit out. I'd stopped for a rest and they were spooked by a damn snake."

The large man gazed into the densest section of the trees. "Are you alone, then?"

"No," Zeke replied. "My partner is out trying to round up the horses."

"Which way did your horses run?" the large man inquired.

Ezekiel pointed to the west. "In the direction I want to go, but unfortunately without me in the saddle." He laughed again. "I'm hoping you'll be kind enough to lend my partner a hand. I hate to be standing about in Indian country."

"I know what you mean," the large man agreed. "My name is Gant, by the way."

"My friends call me Zeke."

"Well, Zeke, we wouldn't want to leave you alone in your time of need. My partner here, Madison, will head out and help your friend while we stay here in case any Indians should show up." Gant nodded at the man on his left, who urged his animal past Zeke and rode off at a leisurely pace.

Nathaniel did not bother to watch the man depart. He

trained his rifle on the larger rider, Gant.

"This is right neighborly of you," Zeke mentioned.

Gant shrugged. "A white man should always look out for another white man, eh?"

"Ain't that the truth."

"Where are you heading?"

"To the Rockies," Zeke revealed.

"Is that a fact?" Gant responded in apparent surprise. "Why, so are we."

"Are you heading for the rendezvous?"

Gant blinked a few times, as if the idea had never occurred to him, then smiled broadly. "We sure are. We hope to get there before all the whiskey is gone. You know how trappers are."

"I guess I do," Zeke said, and studied the men and their mounts. "Are you trappers?"

"How did you guess?" Gant replied jokingly.

"Where are your traps?"

Gant seemed to tense. "What?"

"It's odd to see trappers without their traps," Zeke remarked, still in his brotherly vein. "For that matter, I'm surprised to see you don't have any pack animals."

"We're living off the land as we go," Gant said stiffly. "Pickings are slim, but we get by. As for our traps, they're stored at our cabin on the Green River."

"The Green River?" Zeke said. "I know that country well. Some prime beaver skins have come out of that vicinity."

"We had us a good season last," Gant mentioned. "Took in near three thousand skins."

Zeke whistled in appreciation. "That's a heap of pelts. What, about a thousand a man?"

"Pretty near," Gant said. "I did a little better than my partners."

"What did you do with your windfall?"

"What else? We've spent the past month in St. Louis doing what comes naturally."

Ezekiel chuckled. "Those St. Louis women know how to treat a man right."

Perplexed by his uncle's friendliness, his nerves frayed to the limit, Nathaniel held the barrel fixed on the large man and wondered what was going on. Why didn't Zeke simply challenge Gant and get it over with? Why were they being so nice when each would just as soon shoot the other? He observed his uncle glance westward, and he risked a hasty look in the same direction. The other rider, Madison, was nowhere in sight. Could that be what Zeke was waiting for?

"I hope they find my horses soon," Zeke commented. "It was my own fault. I should have tied them up."

"You know what they say," Gant responded. "Count ribs or count tracks."

Now what in the world did that mean? Nathaniel speculated. His skin felt clammy and cold.

"Care for some jerky?" Gant asked.

"Don't mind if I do."

The large man climbed down and stuck his right hand in a blanket tied behind his saddle.

Nathaniel saw Ezekiel get a firmer grip on his rifle. He braced for the worst, thinking that Gant would pull a pistol from the blanket. Instead, out came a wide strip of jerky.

"Here we go," the large man stated. He wedged his rifle between his legs and drew his knife, then proceeded to cut several pieces of dried meat from the strip and handed a morsel to Zeke.

"I thank you kindly."

"We have some to spare in case you don't find your pack animal."

Hidden by the trees and the grass, Nathaniel listened attentively. He shifted his aim from the large man to the one still in the saddle. Zeke and Gant were now two yards apart, and he counted on his uncle to handle Gant when the time came. *If* it ever came.

"All this kindness has me a mite confused," Ezekiel said while chewing on the jerky.

"Why's that?" Gant replied.

"Because if you're aiming to rob and kill a man, you ought to come right out and do it instead of talking him to death."

Nathaniel suddenly felt light-headed. His uncle had thrown

down the gauntlet, and if Gant and the other man were innocent of any wrongful intent they were bound to become rather mad. But if they were, as Zeke asserted, cutthroats, how would they react? He received an answer an instant later when Gant went for his gun.

# Chapter Ten

It all happened so incredibly fast.

Nathaniel saw the mounted man snap a rifle up, and without any regard for the consequences, thinking only of his uncle's safety, he sighted on the man's chest and squeezed the trigger. The boom of the Hawken produced a cloud of smoke and slapped the butt plate against his right shoulder.

A surprised grunt came from the rider as the ball bored through his torso and knocked him from his horse.

Ezekiel and Gant were bringing their rifles to bear, and Zeke was a shade quicker. He fired, the ball striking the larger man high in the chest and causing Gant to stumble backwards and drop to one knee.

Alarmed, well aware that both men could still pose a threat, Nathaniel released his rifle, scooped up his pistols, and sprinted toward the river bank. Zeke had already drawn his pistol and fired into Gant's chest, and this time the big man toppled onto his back.

Just then, while Zeke held his smoking pistol trained on Gant, the other rider stepped unsteadily into view near the head of his skittish horse. He pointed his rifle, the barrel swaying from side to side.

"Uncle Zeke!" Nathaniel cried, his fear lending Mercury's wings to his feet, running as he had never run before, and his shout served a twofold purpose.

Ezekiel frantically threw himself backwards, out of the line of fire.

The rider hesitated, swinging in the direction of the yell, still unable to hold the barrel straight.

Again Nathaniel gave no thought to the repercussions of his act. He extended both arms and fired while on the run, figuring at such close range he was bound to hit his target. And he did.

The robber staggered as a ball smacked into his right side, piercing the flesh and shattering a rib bone, even as the second ball struck him at the base of the throat, passed clear through his neck, and shattered the top of his spine. His arms waving wildly, spitting blood as he gurgled, he reeled backwards and tumbled into the river with a loud splash.

Nathaniel reached his uncle's side and halted, staring in disbelief at the pair of motionless bodies. "Dear Lord," he gasped. "What have I done?"

"We're not finished yet," Ezekiel said. He was reloading his rifle, his hands flying, and glancing repeatedly to the west.

"We're not?" Nathaniel asked, not quite comprehending, his arms still extended, breathing in the acrid gun smoke.

"No," Zeke reiterated, ramming a ball home.

And suddenly Nathaniel remembered the man who had ridden off to assist in rounding up the fictitious strays. He swung around and spied a lone rider galloping toward the stand of trees, a rifle held aloft, 300 yards distant.

"Keep coming, you son of a bitch," Zeke said, raising the rifle to his shoulder.

Nathaniel opened his mouth to protest, then changed his mind. What good would it do? His uncle had no intention of letting the man live, and who was he to dispute Zeke? Which one of them knew best how to survive on the frontier? Certainly not him with his New York City upbringing, which had emphasized living by the rules of polite society, according to the structured laws of civilization. He glanced at the dead man in the river, who was floating within inches of the bank. What rules prevailed here? Survival of the fittest? Civilization lay far to the east, and the laws imposed by those in power no longer applied. Out here, out in the untrammeled wilderness, every man appeared to be a law unto himself.

"Keep coming," Zeke repeated.

Lowering his arms, Nathaniel looked to the west. The third man was now only 200 yards off, racing toward them, evidently oblivious to the fact his companions were dead. Couldn't he see them? Didn't he—

The sharp crack of Zeke's rifle punctuated Nathaniel's thought, and the onrushing rider suddenly swayed in the saddle, then toppled off his horse, landing headfirst, his rifle sailing through the air to clatter a dozen yards from his lifeless form.

"Got him," Ezekiel stated happily, and lowered his Hawken. "So much for those three."

"We killed them," Nathaniel said softly.

Zeke nodded. "We sure as hell did. It was either them or us, nephew. And I'm right proud of the job you done."

"I shot a man," Nathaniel said lamely.

"And a smart rifle shot it was," Zeke stated, and clapped the young man on the back. "I couldn't have done any better. And the way you finished him off with the pistols!" He laughed heartily. "You're a natural-born fighter."

Nathaniel looked at Gant and saw blood oozing from the big man's chest. "Should I be proud of the fact?" he asked.

"Certainly," Ezekiel responded, at work loading his rifle once again. "You're proven you're a man after all, not one of those dandified sissies the cities breed like rats."

"I don't feel very manly," Nathaniel divulged, striving to come to terms with his feelings. "I feel . . . strange," he said, for want of a better word.

"It'll pass, nephew," Zeke assured him. "I felt the same way when I killed my first man. But the feeling goes away. Eventually you'll regard the killing of a bad man in the same light as killing any vermin."

"I will?" Nathaniel responded, and the notion shocked him. If he ever became that callous, what would serve to distinguish him from the lower animals?

"We must each live according to our nature, Nate," Zeke said solemnly. "There's no getting around the fact. Try, and you're doomed for a life of misery."

A listless sensation crept through Nathaniel's veins, and he regarded his pistols as if they were alien objects he'd never beheld before. "What is my nature?" he queried absently.

"That's what I hope you'll discover before this treasure hunt of ours is over," Zeke said. "Now you'd best reload your guns in case any unfriendly sorts heard our shots."

"Unfriendly sorts?"

"Indians, nephew. Indians."

Nathaniel needed no further prompting. The thought of hostile Indians dispelled his moodiness, and he hastily retrieved his rifle and reloaded all three guns. Once the pistols were again secure under his leather belt and he had his rifle grasped firmly in his hands, he turned to his uncle.

Zeke was already busily at work. He had hauled the dead rider from the river and aligned the body next to Gant's. Then he had stripped each man of their guns, knives, powder horns, and bullet pouches. Now he was about to mount Gant's sturdy animal.

"Do you want me to bury them?" Nathaniel queried.

The question gave Zeke pause. He glanced over his shoulder. "Whatever for?"

"So the beasts don't devour them."

"Why deprive the beasts of a meal?"

Nathaniel envisioned a pack of wolves tearing into the corpses, and swallowed. "But that's not proper."

"Why do you think the Good Lord created vultures? It's not proper to deprive the buzzards of their meal. So just drag the bodies into the trees and we'll leave them there."

"Just like that?"

"Nephew, I wasn't joking about Indians. I've seen sign of some in this vicinity, and I don't mean Otos. Now get cracking." So saying, Zeke mounted and rode toward the third corpse.

Nathaniel gazed skyward, his soul in torment. He'd killed! Violated one of the Ten Commandments! So what happened now? Would he spent eternity in Hell, tortured for the deed he had done? Or would a bolt of lightning flash from the clear sky and fry him to a cinder? He scanned the heavens, almost disappointed when nothing transpired. Yes, he had killed, but the world went on. The sun still shone and birds still sang and fish swam in the river. Was the passing of a human life of such inconsequence, then? Bothered by his train of thought, he shook his head and propped his rifle against a nearby tree. Working laboriously, he dragged the man he'd shot deep into the cedar trees, then returned for Gant.

Ezekiel was riding up with the third man's horse in tow and the robber's body draped over the saddle. "Wait until I tell Shakespeare about this," he said, in high spirits. "He'll enjoy a laugh at the way I skunked these scoundrels."

"Skunked them?"

"Didn't you hear me?" Zeke asked, dismounting. "Oh, that's right. You wouldn't have understood. Nephew, those men weren't trappers. They were fixing to kill us for my gold. I tricked them into confessing as much."

"How?"

"By getting them to talk about their so-called trapping activities. Did you hear the big one tell me they caught three thousand beaver in a season?"

"Yes."

"That came to a thousand per man."

"So?"

"So there ain't a man alive who has caught one thousand beaver in a single season. It's not humanly possible. Why, Jeb Smith himself caught only six hundred and sixty-eight in a whole year, not just one season."

Nathaniel had heard of Jebediah Smith, who in 1826 had led a party of fur trappers from the Great Salt Lake all the way to the Mission San Gabriel in California, the first to successfully do so. "How many seasons are there?" he queried.

"Two. The first is in the fall when the fur has reached its prime and runs until the ice makes trapping out of the question. The second starts in springtime and goes until about June, when the warm weather means the fur is real thin."

"Do you know Jeb Smith?" Nathaniel thought to inquire.

"I've met him a few times," Zeke disclosed. "He's got the mountains in his blood, and every mountain man in the wilderness recognizes him as one of the best who ever lived. And did you know he's only around twenty-eight years old?"

"No, I didn't," Nathaniel confessed. "Somehow, I figured he would be older."

Zeke locked his eyes on his nephew. "Out here, Nate, it's not a man's years that count. It's his experience. You're only nineteen. Why, if you were of a mind to stay out in the west, you could be as highly regarded as Jeb Smith by the time you're twenty-eight."

"Stay out here?" Nathaniel said, and snorted at the idea. "Not when I have Adeline waiting for me."

Ezekiel's fine spirits abruptly dissipated. "That's right. I plumb forgot about Adeline."

"I never will," Nathaniel vowed.

Zeke turned to the body draped over the horse. "Give me a hand."

Together they dragged the man named Madison into the brush with his fellows, then covered all three with limbs and greenery.

"Why go to all this bother if the vultures are going to eat them?" Nathaniel asked.

"The scavengers will find them soon enough. In a few days they'll be ripe enough to draw flies and coyotes from miles around. In the meantime, we want to put as much distance between them and us as we can. And we don't want anyone to find them right away," Zeke explained.

They walked back to their horses.

"What will we do with their animals?" Nathaniel questioned.

"What do you think? We'll keep them."

"We just take their animals? Doesn't that make us the same as the men we killed?"

"No."

"Why not?"

Zeke chuckled. "We're alive. They're not."

They mounted and rode westward, Ezekiel leading three

horses, Nathaniel only two. Except when spoken to, for the next five days Nathaniel hardly uttered a word, immersed in reflection on his part in the slayings of the would-be gold robbers. Zeke kept to himself, recognizing his nephew's agitated state of mind and respectfully allowing the youth to sort the matter out, vividly recalling how he'd felt when he killed his first foe.

On the fifth day, as he lay on his blanket not far from their smoldering fire, gazing in awe at the celestial display overhead, dazzled by the sheer number of stars, Nathaniel came to terms with himself. Since he wanted to return to Adeline at all costs, and since he wouldn't be able to see her again if he was dead, he logically concluded that staying alive was a foremost priority. And since in this great, sprawling wilderness where the men were often every bit as savage as the beasts they were trying to subdue, killing for food or simply in self-defense was an accepted practice, then if he was forced to kill to preserve his life, so be it. He believed his Maker would judge him in mercy and with compassion. And surely the Lord didn't intend for a man to stand idly by while another took his life! With such thoughts of personal absolution soothing his soul, he drifted into peaceful slumber.

The next morning the warmth of the rising sun on his upturned cheeks roused Nathaniel to wakefulness, and he sat up to discover his uncle already awake and packing their gear.

"Well, sleepyhead, it's nice to see you're not going to sleep the day away," Zeke joked.

"How do you do it? No matter how early I rise, you're always up before me," Nathaniel commented, rubbing his eyes and yawning.

"Life is meant for living, nephew. I don't believe in wasting a minute. I've trained myself to wake at the first streak of light on the eastern horizon. You might practice doing the same."

"I'll try," Nathaniel said halfheartedly.

Ezekiel grinned. "Why don't you splash some life into you, Nate?"

Nodding, Nathaniel rose and shuffled toward the Republican River, a distance of 30 yards. They had taken shelter for the night in a small clearing in the center of a ring of trees and scrub brush. His moccasins crunched on twigs as he ambled along. Still fatigued, his body sluggish to respond to the demands of a new day, he traversed the 30 yards in a daze. Only when he reached the south side of the river and knelt to dip his hands in the chilly water did he finally come to his full senses. And even then the water had nothing to do with his rude awakening. It was the guttural growl that emanated from off to his left, and the huge brute he spied when he swung in that direction.

Not 25 feet away, illuminated in all its primal ferocity by the increasing sunlight, stood an enormous grizzly bear.

# Chapter Eleven

Stark, unadulterated terror welled within Nathaniel's breast at the sight of the monster. His mind and body were suddenly numb; he couldn't think, couldn't will himself to move, and he stayed there on his knees with his fingers in the water while the bruin lumbered slowly toward him.

Seven feet in length from the tip of its nose to its bobbed tail and weighing over 1200 pounds, the grizzly loomed in the dawn like one of the prehistoric mammoths unearthed in New York 20-odd years ago. Rippling with powerful muscles and steely sinews, the telltale hump bulging between its massive shoulders, the bear drew nearer and nearer, swinging its extremely wide head from side to side and sniffing the cool air. Its coat was primarily brown, but all the hairs were white-tipped, giving the beast its grizzled aspect.

Nathaniel finally recovered his presence of mind and glanced toward the camp. There was no sign of Ezekiel, and if he yelled to attract his uncle the bear might charge. He looked down at his belt, thinking of the pistols and rifle he had left lying next to his blanket, and chided himself for being so stupid as to traipse off without a gun.

The grizzly bear was now only 15 feet away.

*What do I do?* Nathaniel mentally screamed. He couldn't just kneel there like a bump on a log and let the bear get within striking range. He could see the grizzly's four-inch claws on its forefeet, and he could well imagine what a swipe from one of those gigantic paws would do to him.

Only 12 feet separated the two.

Girding his courage, Nathaniel abruptly stood erect, his hands at his sides, and faced the bear.

The grizzly drew up short, raising its head and sniffing even louder.

Nathaniel's mind raced as he debated the wisest course of action. Should he stand still and hope the bear would leave, or should he make a run for it? And if he ran, should he head for the camp and shout for his uncle, hoping he was fleeter of foot than the bruin? Or should he retreat into the river where the bear might not follow? Did grizzly bears like to enter water? Ezekiel had told him all about deer and antelope and elk and other animals, but never once had Nathaniel thought to inquire about bears for the simple reason he hadn't seen any. Until now.

Without any warning of its intent, the colossal grizzly reared upright, its front paws held with the claws extended, its mouth hanging wide to reveal its long, sturdy teeth. The beast growled again.

His fear getting the better of his reason, Nathaniel instinctively backed away from the bear, retreating into the shallow water at the edge of the river.

The grizzly dropped onto all fours and ponderously advanced, rumbling deep in its chest, its eyes fixed on the man.

Nathaniel could stand the strain no longer. He cupped his hands to his mouth and bellowed at the top of his lungs. "Zeke! A grizzly!" Then he retreated several more strides. His left hand bumped a hard object on his hip, and all of a sudden he remembered the 12-inch hunting knife he carried. He drew the blade with his right hand and held the weapon at waist level. Compared to the size of the mighty bruin, the hunting knife seemed puny indeed, but it was all he had and he refused to go down without a fight.

The shout prompted the grizzly to growl louder, and it stepped to the river's edge, then hesitated for a moment.

Nathaniel glanced over the bear's back, and his hopes soared when he spotted his uncle sprinting toward the Republican, a rifle in each hand. He began to think he would survive his first encounter with a grizzly without receiving so much as a scratch, that perhaps the reputation of the species for ferocity was vastly overestimated, when the bear proved him wrong.

The grizzly attacked.

Nathaniel's eyes widened as the bear waded into the Republican, splashing water in all directions, and came for him, its enormous jaws opening and closing. He frantically backed farther away, until the water rose to his waist, and thinking that he might be safer if he could reach the opposite shore, he spun and was about to swim for it when the unexpected occurred. He slipped, his left moccasin sliding off an unseen rock underwater, and stumbled forward a pace, sinking onto his left knee, the water rising almost to his chin.

A bestial growl sounded right behind him.

Panic gripping him, Nathaniel straightened and whirled and found himself staring straight into the eyes of the horrendous brute. A paw streaked out of nowhere and caught him on the left shoulder, the claws ripping his buckskin shirt and tearing into his flesh, and the force of the blow knocked him backwards. He nearly lost his footing and went under, his arms swinging wildly, but at the last instant he regained his balance and surged erect.

And there was the grizzly, coming at him again, its gaping maw about to bite.

Nathaniel twisted and sidestepped to the right. His left shoulder throbbed and his entire arm arched. Ignoring the agony, he swung his right hand in an arc, striking in frenzied desperation, and stabbed the bruin in the head. Once, twice, three times he struck, and the third time the blade speared into the grizzly's left eye and held fast in the socket. Before he could wrench the knife free, a reverse swipe of the bear's paw connected with his chest and sent him sailing into the river. He went under, forgetting to close his mouth, and water poured down his throat. *I'm drowning!* he thought, and thrashed his legs, seeking a firm footing, completely disoriented. His moccasins found a purchase on the bottom and he pushed upward, his head breaking the surface, the water up to his chin. He sputtered and gasped, then stiffened when he saw the grizzly not six feet away.

The bear had reared onto its hind legs again, and was uttering the most savage sounds while shaking its head and pawing at the knife imbedded in its socket.

Nathaniel braced for another attack, when to his astonishment the bruin dropped onto all fours, turned, and made for the shore, continuing to vigorously sweep its head to the right and the left, as if the agitated motion might cause the knife to slip out and end its agonized torment. No sooner had all four feet touched solid ground, however, than a solitary shot rent the morning air and the grizzly pitched onto its face, then rolled onto its right side and was still.

"Nate! Nate! Did he get you?"

Dazed by the attack, feeling oddly sluggish, Nathaniel glanced to the right and spied his uncle, a smoking Hawken in his hands. He moved forward, keenly desirous of reaching the bank, afraid he might pass out.

Ezekiel had placed his Hawken on the ground and picked up the second rifle he'd carried from the camp, a gun that formerly belonged to Gant. He warily stepped over to the grizzly and poked its head with the barrel. After satisfying himself that the brute was indeed dead, he laid the rifle down and came into the water to assist his nephew. He saw the torn buckskin shirt and blood trickling down, and swore. "Damn! He did get you!"

Nathaniel heard the words, but they were strangely distorted. He blinked and swallowed, struggling to stay alert, and took one leaden stride after another. A moment later strong arms gripped him under the arms and he felt himself being propelled to the gently sloping bank.

"I have you, Nate," Zeke said. "We'll have that shirt off in no time."

"Is it really dead?" Nathaniel mumbled, staring at the beast in disbelief.

"As dead as they come," Zeke assured him.

"Thanks," Nathaniel said weakly.

"For what? You did most of the work. He was on his last legs when I shot him."

They reached the shore and Ezekiel gently deposited Nathaniel on the ground not six feet from the bear. "Let's remove that shirt," he suggested, and squatted to help remove his garment.

His fingers seemingly composed of mush, Nathaniel fumbled with his belt. Dizziness assailed him, and he was worried he might humiliate himself by fainting.

"I'll do it," Zeke offered, and quickly undid the belt.

Nathaniel left the task to his uncle. He struggled to comprehend why everything was distorted, why he couldn't concentrate. Had he lost too much blood? Would he die here on the prairie? Would Adeline mourn his passing when she learned the news? His head sagged and he saw the bear, the knife jutting from its ruptured eye, blood flowing over its facial fur. Did *I* do that? he marveled. "Dumb luck," he muttered.

"By the Eternal, I only know of one other man who has killed a grizzly with a knife," Zeke declared proudly while stripping off the shirt. He raised Nathaniel's head into his lap so he could slide the soggy buckskin over his nephew's head. "Wait until the word gets out! I'll tell Shakespeare and he'll tell everyone else in the Rockies. That man can gab up a storm."

Nathaniel closed his eyes and breathed deeply, relieved the queasy sensation was subsiding. He debated whether he should look at the wound. The horrible sight of so much gore might be more than his shattered senses could handle.

"Nephew, you are the luckiest man who ever lived. All you've got is a little scratch," Zeke stated, lowering Nathaniel's head.

Surprised, Nathaniel opened his eyes and glanced at his left shoulder. The "scratch" turned out to be three claw marks, three neat incisions in his flesh, the longest several inches in length, starting just below his collarbone and extending to where his arm joined the shoulder. The furrows were no more than half an inch deep and there was scant blood in evidence.

"I'll have you on your feet in an hour," Zeke predicted.

Nathaniel looked up at him. "An hour? Couldn't I rest until at least noon?"

"Whatever for? If you were seriously injured I'd let you rest, but these tiny cuts are hardly worth the bother of patching together."

"Tiny cuts?" Nathaniel retorted indignantly.

Zeke nodded. "Compared to some folks I've see who were attacked by a grizzly, you came off in fine form. Why, once about seven years ago it was, a Canadian trapper I knew stumbled on a she-bear and her cubs. Before he knew what hit him, that bear rammed into him and started ripping him to pieces with her teeth and her claws. By the time she was done, his legs were nearly severed from his body and the right side of his face had been chewed to the bone."

The queasy sensation returned and Nathaniel blanched. "I'd rather not hear about it, if you don't mind."

"Grizzlies are the most unpredictable critters the Good Lord ever put on the face of this earth," Zeke went on philosophically. "You never know if they'll turn tail or try to eat you, and they can be regular devils to kill when their dander is up. I've known of grizzlies who were shot ten to fifteen times and they still wouldn't keel over. Take my word for it. You want to avoid grizzly bears at all costs."

Nathaniel almost laughed. "I'll try to keep it in mind," he said dryly.

Ezekiel grinned and studied his nephew's face for several seconds. "There. I guess you're out of your shock. Now stay put while I go to camp and fetch my bag. But first—" he said, and rose. In seconds he was back with Gant's rifle. "Hold onto this in case your bear has a friend lurking about."

"A friend?"

"Sometimes they roam in pairs. Not often, but sometimes," Zeke said. He hurried off, retrieved his Hawken and ran toward their camp.

Gritting his teeth, Nathaniel used his right elbow to prop himself off the ground, then straightened in a sitting posture. He wasn't about to lay on his back when there might be another of those monsters in the vicinity. A survey of his surroundings assured him he was alone, and he expelled a breath in relief. The dead bear drew his attention. How could he have survived an attack from such an awesome creature? If he hadn't actually lived through the experience, he would doubt such a feat was possible.

Something caused a splash in the river.

Startled, Nathaniel stared at the Republican, but all he saw were ripples on the water. A fish, he figured, and happened to gaze at the plain beyond the Republican. The figure he spotted less than 100 yards away prompted him to leap to his feet in astonishment, momentarily forgetting all about the bear and his shoulder wound, forgetting everything except the man astride the horse.

An Indian.

He sat astride his horse in an attitude of casual curiosity, wearing only a breechcloth and moccasins. Over his back hung a quiver of arrows. In his left hand he held a short bow. His dark hair hung down on both sides of his head to his naked shoulders.

Nathaniel started to raise the rifle, then thought better of the idea. The Indian had not displayed any hostility, and he doubted his uncle would be pleased if he shot a friendly warrior. So he simply returned the other's stare and waited for the Indian to make the first move.

After a minute the warrior made a gesture with his right hand, then nodded and wheeled his mount. Without a backward glance he rode to the north, sitting tall and easy, riding bareback. Soon he was out of sight, disappearing in a small cluster of trees far off.

Abruptly feeling weak, Nathaniel sank to his knees and

pursed his lips. There was so much he had yet to learn about
life in the West, he wondered if he would live long enough
to learn it all. He had no idea to which tribe the Indian might
belong; for all he knew, the warrior might return with others
of his tribe to slay Zeke and him. He began to realize that
making a mistake in the wilderness, even the smallest, most
inconsequential error such as leaving camp without a gun,
could have a fatal outcome. How different life here was from
New York City, where a man could leave his house forgetting
to take along one of his personal effects, such as his overcoat,
and experience nothing more than a minor inconvenience.
Apparently civilization cushioned people from the harsher
realities of life.

"Here we go."

Nathaniel shifted, relieved to find his uncle returning so
quickly. "I saw an Indian," he blurted.

Ezekiel halted in midstride and scanned the surrounding
expanse of grass and flowers. "Where?"

"There," Nathaniel said, and pointed. "He watched me
for a bit, then rode off."

"Describe him."

"He was sort of tall and had a bow and arrows," Nathaniel
replied, uncertain as to which details his uncle wanted to
know. There wasn't many he could provide, in any event.
"I don't know what else to say."

"Was his hair shaved?"

"No. Why?"

"If his hair had been shaved except for a strip from the
forehead to the neck, then he would have been Pawnee. Their
villages are north of us a ways. They don't give white men
much trouble," Zeke said, and frowned. "But since his hair
wasn't shaved, then my guess is the warrior was part of a
Cheyenne war party. The area we're in is at the eastern edge
of their territory."

"Are the Cheyenne friendly?"

"Sometimes yes. Sometimes no."

"That's not very reassuring."

"It's not meant to be," Ezekiel said, and squatted

alongside his nephew. "I'll dress those cuts and we'll be on our way. If there is a Cheyenne war party hereabouts, we want to get somewhere else as fast as we can." He paused and grinned. "I'm rather fond of my scalp and I hope to keep it a spell."

# Chapter Twelve

Ezekiel followed the Republican for another two miles, then struck a course to the northwest, pushing the horses, his alert gaze constantly roving over the prairie. He repeatedly glanced over his shoulder, watching their back trail.

His left shoulder throbbing, Nathaniel was hard pressed to keep up. He looked forward with keen anticipation to stopping for the night so he could rest. The thought of nine or ten more hours in the saddle did not appeal to him in the least.

After they had traveled four miles, Ezekiel relaxed a bit and slowed down. "I don't see any sign of pursuit," he announced.

"Good. Maybe we can stop soon and take a break," Nathaniel suggested.

"Not on your life. Not until we've put a goodly distance between any Indians and us."

Nathaniel was holding the reins in his right hand. His left arm he held bent at the elbow and tucked in to his side, with the Hawken barrel wedged into the crook of his arm. Carrying the rifle was painful, but he wasn't about to ride unarmed through country brimming with hostile Indians. He started a conversation to take his mind off his discomfort. "Have you ever killed a grizzly bear?"

"More times than I could count."

"And you were never hurt?"

"A few nicks and bites," Zeke disclosed. "I know as much about grizzlies as any man living, I reckon, except for Shakespeare. So pay attention. Grizzlies might be unpredictable, but they'll usually leave a man alone unless you get too close or it's a she-bear with cubs. *Never* go near a bear with cubs. You're just asking for trouble." ·

"Why didn't that bear leave me alone? I did nothing to provoke it, yet it kept coming closer and closer and sniffing as if it liked my scent."

"There's the key. Your scent. Grizzlies live by their nose. They go from scent to scent like a butterfly from flower to flower, looking for something tasty to eat. Shakespeare says a grizzly doesn't have the best eyesight in the world, but it damn sure has the best nose," Zeke said, and chuckled. "There's a saying the trappers have about the grizzly. If a pine needle falls in the woods, the eagle will see it, the deer will hear it, and the bear will smell it. Nine times out of ten, when a bear gets your scent, it'll head for the hills. But if the wind is blowing your scent away from the bear, or if you surprise it, then watch out."

"Do you think the bear that attacked me had my scent?"

"Hard to say, nephew. But I suspect the bear was more curious about you than crazed with the killing lust, or you wouldn't be alive right now."

"The next time I see one I'll run like hell," Nathaniel mentioned, thinking of the advice Zeke had given him concerning Indians.

"That's one thing you never want to do with a bear."

"No?" Nathaniel asked in surprise.

"Not unless the bear is already after you. Grizzlies are as thick as fleas on a mangy dog in some parts of this country. You'll be running into them all the time, so you'd better learn the basics now. If a grizzly does come after you, hold your ground. Face the bear down. Most of the time they'll run up to within a few yards of you, stand up, and glare into your eyes, as if they're taking your measure. If you run, they'll chase you and tear you to pieces. This advice holds for most any critter in God's creation. The Good Lord made us to be the masters of the brutes, and most beasts won't attack unless you show cowardice," Zeke asserted.

Nathaniel digested the information thoughtfully. So he had committed two blunders that morning. The first was leaving the camp without his rifle, which he would never do again. And the second had been in retreating from the bear and entering the river.

"Actually, the same advice holds true for Indians," Ezekiel went on. "Never let on that you're afraid of them or you'll be sorry. The Indians respect bravery above all else. That's why they attach so much importance to counting *coup.*"

"To what?"

"*Coup,* Nate. Counting *coup* is how an Indian warrior proves his manhood. For a warrior to win glory, he has to touch his enemy. Each time he does, he counts *coup.* Some of the tribes even have special sticks for just that purpose."

"I don't get it," Nathaniel ssid. "What's so important about touching an enemy?"

"The way the Indian looks at war, it takes no great courage to kill an enemy from afar, to shoot him with a bow or a rifle from a hundred yards away. But it does take considerable courage to face an enemy up close and strike him with a hand or a stick or a lance," Zeke explained. "That's why the bravest warriors are always those who have counted the most *coup.*"

"I had no idea. I thought they just killed for the sheer sake of killing."

Ezekiel looked at his nephew. "Indians might be savage, but they're not savages, no matter what you've read in the press."

"You sound as if you admire them."

"There's a lot to admire about the Indian way of life. You'll discover the truth for yourself."

"I will?"

Zeke nodded and rode a little faster.

Two hours later they came to a brook and halted to refresh their horses. A few cedar trees grew near the water's edge, and Nathaniel sat down and leaned his back against one of them, relieved to be sitting still.

Zeke stared to the east, his hand over his eyes, peering intently at the horizon.

"Have any of your friends ever been killed by Indians?" Nathaniel inquired.

"Why do you ask?"

"Just curious."

"Yes, I've lost a few to Indians. The Blackfeet ambushed three of my closest friends near the Jefferson Fork of the upper Missouri River about a year and a half ago. Shot two of them so full of arrows they looked like porcupines. The third they tortured, then scalped."

"How did you find out about it?"

"The third man, Grignon, was released because they couldn't make him cry out even under the worse torments they could devise. So they sent him packing, stark naked, without so much as a knife. They told him to warn all whites to stay away from their land or else."

"What happened to your friend?"

"He stumbled into the camp of another group of trappers about three days later, his feet torn to ribbons, on his last legs. They tried to save him but there was little they could do. He died after two days."

Nathaniel blinked a few times. "Wait a minute. He was still alive after being scalped?"

"Losing your hair doesn't kill you, Nate. It's what happens to you before or after that'll determine whether you live or die."

"How horrible."

"There are worse fates than being scalped."

"I can't imagine what they could be," Nathaniel commented, and closed his eyes. He imagined what it would be like to lose his own hair, and the prospect revolted him.

"Actually, being killed by Indians is just one of the hazards of living in the wilderness. Two years ago one hundred and sixteen men left Santa Fe to trap the southern Rockies and other parts. Only sixteen came back."

Nathaniel straightened. "Sixteen? What happened to the rest?"

"Some were probably killed by Indians. Some likely died from disease. Others were snake-bit or mauled by a grizzly. There are all sorts of things that can happen to a man living in the mountains."

"Why would anyone want to put up with such hardships just to live in the wilderness?"

Zeke sighed. "That's a question many a man has asked himself. The answer might surprise you."

"I don't intend to stay out here long enough to learn the answer."

"You never know, nephew."

Nathaniel closed his eyes and thought of Adeline. Spending a year away from her, spending 12 whole months in the mountains with his uncle, appealed to him less and less with each passing day. The farther they went, the more convinced he became that it would be a miracle if he lived to see his sweetheart again. True, he wanted to be rich, but was wealth worth his life? Was Adeline's love worth such a cost? Was he—

"Nate!"

The harsh word brought Nathaniel out of his reverie. He opened his eyes and saw his uncle gazing at a distant point to the east. "What is it?"

"Get mounted. There are Indians on our trail."

Even with his injured shoulder, Nathaniel climbed on his horse faster than he ever had before. The pain was momentarily forgotten in the urgency of the moment.

Zeke stared eastward for a few more seconds, then mounted and headed due west, crossing the shallow brook.

"Are they Cheyenne?" Nathaniel asked, riding on his uncle's left.

"They're too far away to tell," Zeke said. "And we don't

want them to get any closer if we can help it.''

They rode hard for 20 minutes, passing several dozen antelope and a solitary wolf that bounded away at their approach. A low hill appeared ahead, not much more than a mound of dirt and wispy grass, yet still the highest elevation for miles around. Ezekiel made straight for the rise and reined up at the top, swinging his roan around.

Nathaniel did the same, and far to the east he saw the band of horsemen coming after them. He counted eight riders, and even to his untrained eye they were clearly not white men.

''Damn!'' Zeke declared angrily. ''We're in for it now.''

''Do we make a stand?''

''Not if I can help it,'' Zeke replied. ''I'd prefer to outrun them, but with all these extra horses we don't stand a prayer.''

''What if we leave the horses we took from Gant and the others here? Maybe the Indians will be satisfied with them,'' Nathaniel proposed.

''I wouldn't count on it. I know one man who tried that trick once, and the Indians took his spare animals and still chased him for over a day. He barely got away with his life.''

''Then what do we do?''

Ezekiel pursed his lips and surveyed the countryside in every direction. For miles around lay rolling prairie, a seemingly endless expanse of thin grass, with not so much as a tree to afford a hiding place. ''I reckon we make that stand after all.'' He slid down and inspected his Hawken.

Nathaniel dismounted and stood regarding the figures on the plain, calculating that the Indians would reach the hill within five minutes at the most.

''If worse comes to worst, we'll shoot the horses we took from those vermin and use them as a breastwork,'' Zeke proposed.

''Shoot the horses?''

''Would you rather have the Indians shoot us? Out here horses aren't pets, Nate. Never become too attached to your animal because you may have to eat it.''

''Never,'' Nathaniel stated, glancing at his mare.

''If you're hungry enough, you'll eat anything,'' Zeke

stated. "And horse meat beats starvation any day."

"I hope I'm never that hungry."

Ezekiel took several paces and cradled his rifle in his arms. "We'll have an advantage over those devils if they try to take us. They'll see just the two of us and expect us to have only two rifles. But we have five, plus our pistols and the extra pistols we took from Gant and his partners." He chuckled. "Yes, sir. We could give those Indians a powerful surprise."

"But what if they all have rifles?"

"Not very likely. Most warriors prefer a bow, lance, or tomahawk to a rifle when it comes to killing. And those who do own rifles are not always the best shots in the world."

"I hope you're right."

"Don't be such a worrywart, Nate. You'll live longer."

Nathaniel absently nodded, but inwardly he felt a gnawing knot of fear at the likelihood of fighting Indians. *Indians!* He had read about the atrocities attributed to the red man, about the scalpings and other revolting horrors allegedly practiced by the barbaric tribes in the vast unexplored lands west of the Mississippi. Never in his wildest dreams had he expected to be contending with them in a fight for his life. What *am* I doing here? he asked himself again and again, watching the warriors draw closer and closer.

"Remember, put on a brave front," Zeke advised.

Troubled, Nathaniel looked at his uncle. "Are you afraid to die?"

"Afraid? No, I wouldn't say that. You grow to accept death as your constant companion out here, Nate. Once you know it can happen at any time, you sort of resign yourself to that fact. Oh, I don't *want* to die, and I'll do my best to stay alive. But no, I can't honestly say I'm afraid right at this moment."

"I am," Nate said softly.

"Fear is nothing to be ashamed of, not so long as you don't let it get the better of you. You can conquer fear with your mind if you give it a try," Zeke said. "Besides, didn't you learn your lesson from what happened with Gant?"

"Which lesson?"

"That when the chips are down, when your life is in danger, when you have no choice but to kill or be killed, your fear evaporates like dew under a hot sun." Ezekiel glanced at the horses. "Fetch the other rifles and pistols and lay them here so they'll be handy when the shooting commences."

Nathaniel hastily complied, and as he deposited the last of the rifles on the ground at his feet he looked up to discover the band of Indians within 500 yards of the hill.

"Damn!" Zeke exclaimed.

"What is it?"

"Those aren't Cheyenne, Nate."

"What are they?"

"Kiowa," Zeke said, almost spitting the word out, his features hardening. "Their usual range is far to the south of here. They must be looking for a Cheyenne camp to raid and they came across us instead."

"Are they friendly?"

"Let me put it this way. Never turn your back on a Kiowa unless you aim to commit suicide."

Nathaniel licked his suddenly dry lips and nervously fingered the trigger on his Hawken.

"There has been bad blood between the Cheyennes and the Kiowas for years," Zeke went on. "They raid each other all the time. The Cheyenne will kill a few Kiowas, so naturally the Kiowas have to strike back." He paused. "Mark my words. Sooner or later the two tribes will declare war, and they might not stop until one or the other has been destroyed."

Listening with only half an ear to the news, Nathaniel anxiously watched the eight Indians ride nearer.

"That's what will do the Indians in, you know," Zeke mentioned thoughtfully.

"What?"

"The fact that they're always so busy killing each other off. They'll never be able to stand together against the whites."

Nathaniel opened his mouth to ask why the Indians should have to band together when there were so few whites west of the Mississippi, but the question died in his throat as the eight warriors abruptly halted. A second later one of the Kiowas rode straight for the hill.

"Remember, Nate," Zeke admonished. "This is your survival that's at stake. Any mistakes now, and you'll wish that bear had got you first."

# Chapter Thirteen

Two hundred yards off the Kiowa slowed his horse to a walk and came on cautiously, a lance held in his right hand.

Nathaniel impulsively raised his rifle to his shoulder, but a firm hand pushed the barrel down again.

"Not yet, Nate," Zeke directed. "This one wants to talk. I'll ride down and see what he wants."

"Is that wise?"

"He won't try anything," Zeke said, walking to his roan. "It won't hurt to find out what he has on his mind." He swung into the saddle and headed down the sloping incline.

For the first time since leaving St. Louis, Nathaniel appreciated how dependent he was on his uncle. If anything happened to Zeke, he wouldn't last a week. His apprehension climbing, he glued his eyes to the two men and held his rifle at chest height, ready to fire if need be. He saw them ride to within ten yards of one another and begin communicating in sign language. Their exchange went on for minutes. Finally, the Kiowa warrior made an angry gesture and turned his horse around, then rode briskly toward his fellows.

Ezekiel returned to the top of the hill.

"What happened?" Nathaniel inquired anxiously.

"I just had the honor of meeting Thunder Rider, a Kiowa warrior of some distinction," Zeke said, climbing down. "He told me, as I suspected, that his raiding party is searching for a Cheyenne camp. He was surprised to find any white men in this vicinity and kept asking me if there are any more about. I don't think he believes there are just the two of us."

"Was that all?"

Zeke frowned. "No. He wanted us to trade our guns for horses."

"What did you tell him?"

"What else? To go eat bear."

"Eat bear?" Nathaniel repeated, perplexed.

"The Kiowas never eat bear meat. It's taboo for them, just like eating a dog is taboo for the Cheyenne. So telling Thunder Rider to go eat bear was the same as telling a white man to go to hell."

"How did he take it?"

"Get set for a fight."

Nathaniel gazed at the Kiowa war party. Thunder Rider was talking to the other warriors and making sharp motions toward the hill. He looked down at the extra rifles on the ground, then at the two pistols tucked under his belt, and pondered the fact that he was about to kill again. At that moment, he fervently wished he had never left New York.

"Here they come," Zeke said calmly.

Thunder Rider and the seven other warriors were riding swiftly toward the hill. They started yelling at the top of their lungs, voicing piercing, wild shouts as they waved their weapons in the air.

"Take your time when you aim," Zeke instructed. "We can't afford to waste a shot."

Nathaniel pressed the Hawken to his shoulder, marveling at how composed his uncle could be under the circumstances. He sighted on one of the warriors and waited for them to get within range. The Kiowas were still over 200 yards out, and he wanted them a lot closer to ensure he wouldn't miss.

Ezekiel's rifle cracked.

One of the charging Kiowas flung his arms out and toppled

from his horse. The others immediately checked their charge and rode to the fallen warrior.

"Maybe that will discourage them," Zeke said, although his tone did not convey much confidence. He began reloading.

"Why do they yell like that?" Nathaniel asked absently.

"Those war whoops? Warriors from different tribes all yell like banshees sometimes. It's supposed to unnerve their enemies."

"It works."

Zeke smiled. "You're doing fine."

"I haven't done anything yet."

"Here's your chance," Zeke stated, and nodded at the Kiowas.

Nathaniel turned, scarcely breathing at the sight of the warriors renewing their attack. Again he took aim, selecting a Kiowa with several feathers in his hair. He held the barrel as steady as he could, trying to compensate for the elevation and the trajectory as his uncle had taught him, afraid his lack of experience would cause him to miss. He was about to squeeze the trigger when the Kiowas adopted a wily strategem.

The warriors suddenly slid onto the sides of their horses, each man lying in a horizontal position along the length of his racing animal, with one heel hanging on the horse's back for support, presenting the smallest possible target.

Ezekiel fired.

Trying to get a bead on the Kiowas, Nathaniel was surprised when none of the Indians fell. His uncle had missed!

"Damn!" Zeke fumed, lowering his Hawken to the ground and grabbing one of the extra rifles. "Go for their horses, Nate! Their horses!"

Kill a horse? Nathaniel hesitated for all of three seconds. He thought of the fate in store for him if those warriors reached the top of the hill, and he aimed the barrel at an onrushing animal and squeezed the trigger.

The horse stumbled and almost went down, and the Kiowa on its back was forced to swing up in order to avoid being tossed onto the ground. The animal recovered, though, and surged onward.

"Keep shooting!" Ezekiel urged, raising a rifle to his shoulder and sighting on the foremost steed. His gun belched lead and smoke, and the horse abruptly catapulted forward, hit the earth hard, and rolled, throwing its rider in the process.

The six other Kiowas came on at full speed, undeterred. As if on an unseen cue, they fanned out and began weaving their mounts from side to side. Slightly more than 100 yards separated the warriors from their quarry.

"Fire, Nate! Fire!" Zeke prompted.

Nathaniel seized one of the other rifles and aimed at the Kiowa on the right, but the constant changing of direction disconcerted him. Just when he had the horse in his sights the animal would change course.

Ezekiel got off his third shot, and the horse he'd targeted went down in a disjointed whirl of legs, mane, and tail. "Cut one down, Nate!" he bellowed. "They'll be on us soon!"

Taking a breath and holding it, Nathaniel risked a shot, and he grinned in delight when the horse on the right seemed to trip over its own hooves and crashed to the ground. His elation was short-lived however.

Four of the Kiowas were almost upon them.

Nathaniel glanced down at his feet and was startled to realize they had fired all of the rifles. He looked at his uncle, who was quickly reloading, then at the charging Indians. Knowing he couldn't possibly reload before the warriors reached them, he discarded his rifle and drew his two pistols. He saw Thunder Rider and the three others angle their animals toward Zeke and him, and he took several steps toward them, determined to buy his uncle time, to sell his life dearly if necessary. He didn't think of Adeline, or the treasure, or of his family back in New York. He didn't think about whether killing was right or wrong. He didn't think about the odds or the danger. All he thought about was slaying those Indians before they slew him, and he focused his total concentration on the warrior in the lead, trained both pistols on the Kiowa, and waited until the Indian was only

15 feet away and had risen to an upright posture before squeezing both triggers.

Both balls struck the Kiowa in the chest and hurled him from his animal to fall flat on his back in the dirt.

And then the three remaining Kiowas were there, two armed with lances, the third with a bow.

Nathaniel dodged to the right as Thunder Rider's horse barreled toward him and the Kiowa tried to impale him on a lance. The point narrowly missed his chest. He turned toward the spare pistols lying six feet away, and as he did he saw his uncle fire a rifle at the warrior armed with the bow at the very same instant the Kiowa released a shaft. To his horror, both men scored a hit.

The Indian flipped backward from his mount and sprawled onto the hill.

Ezekiel staggered as the arrow penetrated his right side, the tip passing completely through his body and slicing out his back. He sank to his left knee, gripping the shaft, his face ashen from the shock.

''Uncle Zeke!'' Nathaniel cried, and took several strides toward his relative, forgetting about the extra pistols.

Ezekiel swung around, his eyes widening. ''Behind you, Nate!''

The warning saved Nathaniel's life. He spun, and not 20 feet distant was the second Kiowa with a lance, the Indian's horse kicking up dirt and grass as it pounded toward him. The Kiowa drew back his right arm to throw his weapon, and Nathaniel threw himself to the left.

Just as the warrior started to hurl his weapon, the sharp retort of a pistol sounded and a ball hit him squarely in the forehead and he toppled backward.

Nathaniel spun, stunned to see that his uncle had gotten off a pistol shot even with an arrow imbedded in him. He ran for the spare pistols, glancing down the hill as he did, consternation seizing him when he beheld two Kiowas sprinting toward the rise on foot. And where was Thunder Rider?

A loud drumming of hooves arose on his right.

Nathaniel looked around in time to see the leader of the

war party closing in on him again, trying to run him through
with the lance. He frantically twisted aside and the lance
missed him by a hair, and as it did his hands flashed out and
took hold of the weapon. Digging in his heels, he held fast
with all of his might, and to his astonishment unhorsed the
warrior.

Thunder Rider fell on his left side, letting go of the lance
as he dropped. Displaying pantherish reflexes, he jumped to
his feet in an instant and drew a tomahawk.

There was no time to try for the pistols. Nathaniel adjusted
his grip on the lance and whipped the point at the warrior.

Strangely, Thunder Rider grinned and bounded forward,
swinging the tomahawk, batting the lance aside.

Nathaniel furiously backpedaled and tried to bring the lance
to bear again, hoping to keep the Kiowa at bay, but Thunder
Rider swatted the lance to the left and pounced. In desperation Nathaniel swept the blunt end of the lance into the
warrior's abdomen, doubling the Kiowa over. He arced the
lance upward, using both arms, and the heavy wood caught
Thunder Rider on the jaw and rocked him backwards.

Somewhere a pistol fired.

An Indian shouted words in the Kiowa tongue.

Ignoring both distractions, Nathaniel reversed his grasp
and speared the point at Thunder Rider's chest.

The warrior evaded the lance, skipping to the right. And
then he did a most peculiar thing. He ignored his intended victim and dashed toward his horse, which had halted a dozen
yards away.

Nathaniel scanned the hill, expecting to find other Kiowas
charging him or attacking Zeke. Instead he saw a lone Kiowa
fleeing on foot down the hill, and the bodies of four warriors
lying nearby.

Thunder Rider leaped astride his horse in a smooth,
graceful motion, and in the blink of an eye he was riding
as fast as he could to the east.

"Nate!"

The agonized dry drew Nate around, and he gasped when
he spotted his uncle doubled over next to the extra pistols.
He ran to Zeke's side and knelt. "I'm here!"

Ezekiel lifted his head. Blood trickled from the right corner of his mouth. "The Kiowa?" he asked faintly.

"We've beaten them. They're leaving," Nate said, staring at the arrow, noting the spreading crimson stain on his uncle's buckskin shirt.

"Sure?" Zeke mumbled, his eyelids fluttering.

"I'm sure," Nathaniel replied, but he glanced over his right shoulder to verify the Kiowas were, indeed, fleeing. He saw Thunder Rider leading a riderless horse to the warrior on foot. Neither was paying any attention to his uncle and himself.

"The others?" Zeke queried, the words barely audible.

"They're all dead, near as I can tell," Nathaniel replied.

"Not the Kiowas," Zeke said, struggling to straighten, his visage contorted in anguish.

"What?"

"The others. Where are the others?" Zeke groaned and almost collapsed.

Nathaniel placed his hands on his uncle's shoulders to keep Zeke from falling. "What others are you talking about?"

The beating of many hooves suddenly filled the air, and over the west rim of the hill rode 15 more Indians.

# Chapter Fourteen

Nathaniel impulsively snatched up two pistols and stood. He stepped around his uncle, placing himself between the Indians and Zeke, and grimly cocked both weapons.

The 15 warriors rode to within a few yards of the Kings and stopped, spread out in a line, staring at the white men without a trace of hostility in their expressions. None went to employ a weapon.

"Come on, damn you!" Nathaniel cried defiantly, flushed with the excitement of the battle and enraged that victory should be torn from him just when he thought the Kiowas had been sent packing. He pointed the pistols at the warrior in the center, who had halted a couple of feet in front of the rest. As he gazed into the Indian's disquieting eyes, recognition dawned.

It was the same one as before.

The warrior he had seen near the Republican.

Close up, the Indian showed a handsome countenance and luxuriant, dark hair. He was muscular and endowed with a robust build. His gaze, even with the pistols trained on him, was unflinching and fearless. Four eagle feathers, not visible previously because of the distance involved, adorned his head.

A hand fell on Nathaniel's leg and he glanced down.

"Don't shoot," Zeke said, still on his knees, staying as straight as he could. "They're not Kiowas."

"They're not?" Nathaniel responded, keeping the pistols extended and ready to fire at the slighest provocation.

"No," Zeke stated. "They're Cheyennes."

The warrior in the center surveyed the hilltop, his eyes lingering on each body, and then he gazed to the east at the rapidly departing pair of Kiowas. He barked a few words. Immediately eight of the Cheyenne lit out in pursuit.

"Lower the guns, Nate," Zeke directed.

"I don't trust them."

"If they'd wanted our scalps, we'd already be dead," Zeke said. "Lower the pistols."

Reluctantly, Nathaniel obeyed.

The Cheyennes began talking amongst themselves in low tones. Finally the warrior in the center stared down at Ezekiel, at the arrow jutting from the frontiersman's torso, and slid to the ground.

Nathaniel tensed and started to raise the pistols.

"Don't!" Zeke said. He grunted and bowed his head, his mouth curled in a grimace.

The warrior stepped up to Ezekiel and squatted. He reached out and gingerly touched the shaft, then leaned to the side so he could see the tip protruding from Zeke's back.

"What can I do?" Nathaniel queried, feeling totally helpless, conscious of the stares of the other Cheyennes.

"Nothing," Zeke replied, looking at the warrior in front of him.

The apparent head of the band made a gesture.

Zeke nodded, his lips compressing.

Before Nathaniel could intervene, while he stared in perplexity at his uncle and the warrior, the Cheyenne clasped the arrow firmly, his hands next to Zeke's chest, and with a short, sharp jerk, he snapped the shaft.

Ezekiel's head reared skyward and his mouth widened, but he didn't utter a sound.

The warrior stood and moved around behind Zeke. He knelt, gripped the protruding section of the arrow just above the triangular metal tip, and slowly pulled the rest of the shaft all the way out. A faint sucking noise announced the arrow's extraction.

Disregarding the Indians, Nathaniel knelt next to his uncle. "There must be something I can do," he offered.

"Not yet," Zeke replied.

The warrior stepped in front of them and began using sign language.

Nathaniel watched his uncle respond sluggishly. A few of the signs Zeke had taught him, but the Cheyenne's hands flew too fast for him to follow the exchange. After a few minutes the warrior glanced at him and smiled. Not knowing what else to do, Nathaniel smiled back.

The Cheyenne touched his own chest, then launched into a series of signs.

"What's he saying?" Nathaniel asked.

"He's thanking you for your part in killing his enemies, the Kiowa," Zeke said softly.

"But you did most of the killing."

"He's also telling you that you're welcome in his lodge any time," Zeke translated. The removal of the arrow appeared to have revitalized him to a small degree, and he observed the warrior while pressing his right elbow against the wound.

"Thank him for me."

Zeke relayed the message, then, surprisingly, grinned. "His name is White Eagle. Remember that, Nate."

"I will."

"He says that he hopes to be able to repay you one day for the favor you've done his people, Grizzly Killer."

Nathaniel glanced at his uncle. "Grizzly Killer?"

"Oh, did I forget to mention that?" Ezekiel said, and grinned again. "White Eagle saw you fight the bear. Grizzly Killer is the name he's given you, and from now on that's how every Cheyenne will know you."

"You're kidding?"

"Nope."

"What do I do now?"

"Leave it to me," Zeke said, and executed more hand signs.

After a bit White Eagle responded, then pointed at Nathaniel and added a few sentences in Cheyenne.

"He says that he believes the Master of Life will guide your footsteps in all that you do, that some men are touched in this way and you are one of them, which is rare in a white. He says he knows this because of the way you defeated the bear, that the Master of Life directed your hand," Zeke translated.

"Who is the Master of Life?" Nathaniel inquired.

"Some of the tribes worship a sort of creator force, a Supreme Being. The best I can interpret it, the closest I can come to the meaning of his words, is to call it the Master of Life."

"Thank him again."

"I have a better idea. Give him one of the extra pistols."

"What?"

"Give White Eagle a gun."

"Are you sure?" Nathaniel responded, balking at the idea of supplying a firearm to an Indian who might later use the gun against a trapper or even a soldier from Fort Leavenworth.

"Which one of us has lived out here for ten years? Which one of us knows these people like the back of my hand?" Zeke asked testily. "Give him a pistol and you'll have a friend for life."

Nathaniel eased the hammer down on both pistols and extended his left arm. "Here. Take this as a token of my friendship."

"You learn fast," Zeke said, grinning.

White Eagle looked at the pistol, then at Nathaniel. He took the weapon and inspected the gun carefully, then slid the barrel under the top of his breechcloth. After a moment's consideration, he reached up and removed one of the eagle feathers from his hair and offered the feather to the younger King.

"Do I take it?" Nathaniel queried.

"You'd better, or he'll be insulted," Zeke said.

Nathaniel took the feather into his right hand and admired the excellent state in which the plume had been preserved. "Thanks," he said, and smiled.

"Put it in your hair," Zeke directed.

"Are you serious?"

"Damn it, Nate. Why must you question everything? An Indian doesn't wear a feather just for decoration. A feather is a badge of distinction, just like the medals given to those in the military. White Eagle is showing his gratitude for the pistol by bestowing a great honor on you. Only warriors who have performed bravely in battle get to wear them."

Nathaniel twirled the quill in his fingers. "How do I attach it?"

"Use your noggin, nephew. Cut a piece of fringe from your shirt and tie the feather to the back of your head."

Aware that White Eagle and the other Cheyenne were watching his every move, Nathaniel drew his knife, trimmed a short length of buckskin fringe from his shirt, and secured the eagle feather to his hair. He felt ridiculous doing so, imagining how heartily Adeline would laugh if she could see him now. But then he pondered the fact that she was about two thousand miles away, that adopting to the frontier style of dress made prudent sense, and that White Eagle must figure the feather was a gift equal in value, or maybe even better in a certain respect, than the pistol. He smoothed the feather down, letting it hang to his neck, and regarded the warrior solemnly. "Again I thank you."

White Eagle nodded and used sign language again, his gaze on Ezekiel.

Zeke answered the warrior.

Annoyed at not being able to understand them, Nathaniel vowed to learn sign language at the first opportunity. He glanced at his uncle's wound, wondering how Zeke could withstand the pain.

With a curt nod, White Eagle turned and mounted his horse. In moments the rest of the band was riding hard to the east after their companions.

Nathaniel sighed, amazed at the encounter, gratified to be

alive. He knelt next to Zeke. "Tell me what to do and I'll take care of you."

Ezekiel nodded at their horses, which had skittishly strayed 40 yards to the southwest during the fight with the Kiowas and were now nipping contentedly at the grass. "First catch them, then we'll tend to me."

The catching proved to be an easy task. Nathaniel caught his horse first, then rounded up his uncle's roan, their pack animals, and the three horses they had taken from Gant and his friends. In short order he was back at his uncle's side.

"Now comes the tough part," Zeke said. He began to peel his shirt off, moving laboriously, grimacing in torment.

"Here. Let me," Nathaniel declared, and assisted in removing the bloodstained garment. The arrow had left a finger-sized hole in the flesh, and both the entry and exit points were rimmed with drying blood.

"I was lucky," Zeke commented. "I don't think it hit an organ and I haven't lost too much blood. Once I cauterize the hole, I should be able to manage."

"How will we do that?"

"Since there isn't enough wood around here for a fire, we'll have to make do. Look in the large bag on my pack animals. You'll find a bottle of whiskey."

Nathaniel did as requested and returned with the bottle. He watched in fascination as his uncle poured a large portion of the contents directly into the hole, and he shuddered when he heard Zeke grunt, thinking of the distress his relative must be suffering.

Ezekiel straightened and held out the bottle. "Here. Pour some down the hole in my back."

His stomach feeling queasy, Nathanial took the whiskey and walked around his uncle.

Zeke bent over to make the job easier. "Try not to spill any. This is a terrible waste of good liquor."

"I didn't know you were a drinking man."

"When I'm in the mood, I can drink anyone else under the table except for Shakespeare."

"I'm looking forward to meeting him," Nathaniel mentioned, and slowly upended the bottle over the exit hole.

Zeke stiffened and snorted.

"It must hurt like the dickens," Nathaniel remarked.

"No worse than having your innards torn out by a grizzly."

"How much should I use?"

"That's enough," Zeke declared, and straightened. He took the bottle and swallowed thirstily.

Nathaniel gazed at the bodies of the Kiowas. "Should I bury them?" he inquired.

"You never bury an enemy, Nate. Leave them for the buzzards and the coyotes. But you can do the scalping, if you want."

"The scalping?" Nathaniel repeated, uncertain if he had heard correctly.

Ezekiel nodded. "Those scalps are ours. We took those Kiowas fair and square, and their hair is worth its weight in gold. You can have the honor."

Emotionally dazed by the suggestion, Nathaniel looked at the corpses, then at his uncle, blinking a few times, seeing his relative in a whole new light. He'd noticed a certain change in Zeke's character as they traveled westward, a subtle hardening, a rougher demeanor than his uncle had exhibited in St. Louis. And now he fully appreciated how much Zeke had changed since the lazy days they had enjoyed back in New York. "I don't think I could," he said.

"Give it a try. It's easy. Just pull up on the hair and insert the tip of the knife under the skin. I've seen Indians take off scalps in two or three swipes."

"No," Nathaniel said firmly. "I won't do it."

"You can't afford to be squeamish out here, Nate. A man does what he has to do."

"But to take a scalp!"

"Indians and whites have been doing it for decades," Zeke said. "Why, at one time bounties were paid for Indian scalps in New York. And the Mexican authorities have put bounties on Apache scalps. Almost every tribe I know of takes the scalps of their enemies. A scalp is a symbol of success, nephew, nothing to be ashamed of."

"I won't do it," Nathaniel reiterated.

Ezekiel struggled to his feet. "Oh, well. I can't expect you to see the light yet. I'll do the scalping." He shuffled to the nearest body and sank onto his right knee, then drew his hunting knife.

Nathaniel watched, aghast, as his uncle took hold of the warrior's hair and sliced the knife into the skin at the top of the forehead. Blood started to flow, and Nathaniel turned away and gazed to the west, in the direction they were heading, wondering if he had made a major mistake in agreeing to accompanying Zeke into the wilderness. After all, how much did he truly know about the man other than the fond memories of his childhood? Or was he merely becoming agitated over nothing? If scalping was a way of life out here, and if he intended to stick it out for the whole year, then he should try and accept the practice. He glanced at the scalping in progress, then shook his head.

Accept such a savage custom?

Never!

# Chapter Fifteen

For someone who had been shot with an arrow, Ezekiel remained in exceptionally high spirits. He recovered quickly. For two days he required frequent stops to relieve the pain, but by the third day he could ride for six hours at a stretch without seeming to be bothered by the discomfort.

Nathaniel became subdued, often riding in silence for miles, moodily reflecting on his situation. He wished he had never departed New York, never left his loved ones, especially Adeline. All he could think about was her. He saw her in his mind's eye in the beautiful splendor of every sunrise and in the radiant hues of each sunset. He felt her gentle touch in the lingering caress of the westerly breeze. And at night he gazed at the sparkling heavens and remembered the many hours they had shared together. He longed to see her again, and only one inducement served to keep him riding ever westward, only one lure drew him like a fish to a hook away from the woman of his dreams.

The treasure.

He thought of the gold often, and idly speculated on the amount he would possess after Zeke gave him his share. On several occasions he attempted to sound his uncle out about the treasure, but Zeke always responded in the same fashion: "Once we're at the Rockies, you'll see the treasure. Be patient."

Easy for him to say.

After five days Nathaniel began to shake off his troubled disposition. They were encountering more and more game the farther west they progressed, and he besieged Zeke with questions about the habits of each animal. He also pestered his uncle to teach him sign language, and he readily learned every gesture Zeke knew. They would practice by conducting conversations in sign language. On one such occasion, a week and a half after the battle with the Kiowas, they were riding over a knoll when Ezekiel abruptly reined up.

"Supper!"

In the act of signing a question concerning White Eagle, Nathaniel halted and stared straight ahead, his eyes widening in astonishment. "I never would have believed it!" he exclaimed.

"There's your buffalo, Nate."

Buffalo there were, thousands and thousands of them, covering the plain for as far as the eye could see. The males stood six feet high at the shoulders, the females slightly less. They were dark brown in color and possessed shaggy manes and scruffy beards. Black horns curved out from their broad, massive heads, with a spread of three feet from horn tip to horn tip. There were a score or so of calves in evidence, distinguished by their diminutive size and their reddish hair.

Nathaniel gaped at the great humped beasts, flabbergasted by the immense brutes and the magnitude of the herd. He saw several of the herd gaze in his direction, but none of them displayed any alarm.

"You're in for the treat of your life," Zeke said. "Leave the pack animals here and come with me." He started forward, his Hawken in his right hand.

"You could pick one off from here," Nathaniel commented, riding on his uncle's left.

"I could, but I won't. Where's your sense of sport? Taking a buffalo from horseback is the thrill of a lifetime."

Nathaniel glanced at a huge bull standing proudly at the front of the herd. "Isn't it dangerous?"

"Only if you're careless. Buffalo are the dumbest brutes in creation. They'll let you run them in circles or off of cliffs. But they're also fierce when riled, and they can gore you or your horse to death in the time it takes to spit."

"I see some of them looking at us."

"They know we're coming, but they haven't figured out what we are yet. We're about three hundred yards away, and buffao have pitiful eyesight."

Nathaniel checked his Hawkin, experiencing an odd commingling of excitement and dread.

"These critters supply everything the Indian needs to live," Ezekiel mentioned. "If the buffalo ever die out, the Indians are finished. Not that it will ever happen. There are millions of the brutes. Did you know that each one of those big males weigh about two thousand pounds?"

"No, I didn't."

"That's a lot of meat on the hoof, and the best-tasting meat on God's green earth."

"What if they charge?"

"Get somewhere else right quick," Zeke said, and angled toward the foremost bull. "There's a trick to killing a buffalo. Their skulls are so thick that trying to shoot one in the brain is a waste of time. Your best bet is to always go for a lung shot. Aim just behind the last rib."

Nathaniel stared at the bull, noting the thickness of its hide. "How do I know where the last rib is located?"

"Once you've skinned and butchered one, you'll know exactly where to find the ribs."

"What do I do in the meantime?"

"Guess.

"Oh. There's one other thing to remember. If you ever come across buffalo that have been butchered by Indians, don't take one of the hearts. The Indians will be extremely upset, and the last thing you want is for a tribe to be out for your blood."

"I don't understand. What do the hearts have to do with

anything?''

''Some of the tribes leave the hearts behind. They think that if they leave the hearts where the buffalo have fallen, it helps the herd to grow so they'll have more buffalo to kill later on.''

Nathaniel envisioned a green field littered with buffalo bones and hearts, and shook his head. Was there no end to the wonders of the West?

''We'll take this bull together,'' Zeke stated. ''You ride on the left, I'll stay on the right. Remember, go for the lungs. And try not to shoot me or my horse by mistake.''

''Are you sure you're up to this?''

''I wouldn't miss your first buffalo kill for the world.''

''But your wound hasn't healed yet.''

''It will eventually. For now, I'll act as if it's already healed,'' Zeke said, grinning. He glanced at Nate. ''Out here, nephew, when you're knocked off a horse you get right back up in the saddle.''

''Meaning?''

''If you roll over and whine and moan every time you're hurt, you won't last a year. You've got to be tough, to think tough. This kind of life is no life for a quitter. I know back in the States a lot of parents spoil their youngsters to the point where the children grow into adults and can't do much of anything because the parents didn't teach much of anything worthwhile. Spoiling breeds weaklings, and out here a man and a woman have got to be as strong as catgut.''

They were drawing nearer to the herd. Some of the bulls snorted and fidgeted nervously, while the cows began to move away.

''The herd will likely stampede as soon as we cut out after that bull,'' Zeke said. ''Keep a tight rein on your horse. If you go down, you could be trampeled to death.''

Nathaniel licked his lips. ''Do you do this often?''

''Every chance I get.''

''And this is your idea of fun?''

''It beats wrestling a grizzly.''

More and more of the herd were moving to the southwest, lumbering rapidly, the calves struggling to keep up with their mothers. The bulls, always more belligerent, gave ground reluctantly.

"Are you ready, Nate?" Zeke asked.

"As ready as I'll ever be."

"Then let's get us some buffalo steak," Zeke said, and uttered a piercing shriek while urging his horse toward the bull he'd selected.

Nathaniel kept abreast of his uncle, his heart seemingly pounding in rhythm to the beating of his mare's hooves. He gripped the rifle and concentrated on the bull, which had suddenly spun and was racing to the southwest with the rest of the herd.

"Get as close as you can before you fire!" Zeke shouted.

Nathaniel barely heard him. Hundreds of buffaloes were now in motion, fleeing mindlessly from two riders they could crush in an instant, and more joined the general rout every second. Evidently if one buffalo bolted, they all did, and the sound made by the drumming of thousands of heavy hooves resembled the booming of thunder during a spring storm. The din climbed to a throbbing crescendo, and the passage of the buffaloes sent a billowing cloud of dust into the air.

Whooping and hollering like an Indian, Ezekiel closed on the bull.

They were fast approaching the herd, and Nathaniel could see the thick haunches and the swaying tails of the tremendous beasts. He inhaled the swirling dust and coughed, then squinted to prevent his eyes from watering. As they narrowed the distance his mare became difficult to control. The sight and noise of so many strange creatures terrified her, but she sped gamely onward.

Ezekiel was cackling and waving his rifle.

Bewildered, Nathaniel continued the chase although every instinct told him it would be infinitely safer if he simply stopped and let Zeke enjoy all the "sport." The bull was now at the trailing end of the herd, but there were other buffaloes bolting along on both sides of him. To get close enough for a shot, Nathaniel would have to ride in between the bull and a cow on the left, and with his mare already excitable and balking at drawing any nearer to the fearsome beasts, maneuvering her was a challenge that demanded all of his attention and riding skill.

Zeke had no such problem. His roan readily plunged into the herd, apparently trained for just such a hunting tactic, and Zeke tried to get a bead on the bull while racing at full speed, a difficult task in itself.

The pounding roar of the fleeing buffaloes and the increasingly dense cloud of dust, combined with the ever-present prospect of being pitched from his horse and gored or trampled, made the initial minutes of the chase a nightmare for Nathaniel. As the pursuit continued, though, he began to think less of the danger and more about the job at hand. After all the trouble he was going to, he wanted that bull, wanted to put a ball into that huge bulk and see the brute crash to the ground. He focused on the beast's body, trying to estimate the point he should aim at.

For over half a mile the chase continued. The major part of the herd was obscured by the dust cloud, but the thudding of the thousands of hooves could be clearly heard.

Ezekiel rode into position first, his roan only four feet from the bull and abreast of its rear legs. He suddenly released the reins, pressed the Hawken to his shoulder, took but a moment to sight the rifle, and fired.

The ball had no effect.

Nathaniel barely heard the crack of the Hawken above the thundering of the herd, but he saw the smoke discharged by the shot and knew his uncle could hardly miss at such close range. He was astonished that the bull appeared to be unaffected, and he goaded his mare closer, held his rifle as tightly against his shoulder as he could under the circumstances, and tried to hold the barrel steady long enough to squeeze the trigger.

The bull gave no sign of slowing.

Although he was impatient to snap off a shot, Nathaniel forced himself to stay calm, to wait for the right moment. So engrossed was he in aiming, that he failed to detect any movement to his left and had no idea the cow had changed position until he felt something brush against his left leg. He glanced down.

The cow was within an inch of his foot!

Nathaniel almost panicked. His mare had edged to within a hand's-breadth of the bull, and now he was riding between both buffalo, hemmed in, trapped with no room to turn or evade those wicked horns if either brute tried to gore him. And sooner or later, if he didn't do something, one of them was bound to go for him or the mare.

What should he do?

The urgent question brought an automatic response born of desperation and intuition. Nathaniel simply lowered the Hawken barrel to the bull's side and squeezed the trigger at the same instant that he kicked at the cow and hauled on the reins, bringing the mare to an abrupt stop.

Without breaking her stride, the cow raced onward.

The bull, however, suddenly slowed to an unsteady walk and shook its massive head from side to side. It tottered, then halted as the rest of the herd sped to the southwest.

Nathaniel sat on his mare not 30 feet from the beast, wondering why the bull had stopped. Maybe, he reasoned, one of the balls had finally taken effect. Only when the buffalo turned toward him did he realize his time would be better spent in reloading than in speculation. He groped for his powder horn.

Too late.

The bull lowered its head, elevated its tail, and charged.

Move! Nathaniel's mind screamed, and he wheeled the mare and took off, unsure of the direction he was going and not really caring. The horrific vision of over two thousand pounds of enraged buffalo bearing down on him filled him with dread and he fled for his life, glancing over his right shoulder.

Amazingly, the bull was gaining!

Nathanial clutched at one of his pistols, doubtful the smaller piece would have enough stopping power to deter the bull. As his hand closed on the walnut grip a shot rang out, and he looked to his left to observe Zeke and the smoking Hawken, then back at the buffalo in time to see the bull go down.

Its bearded chin sagging and tucking underneath its head,

the buffalo executed a forward rolling flip, its legs and tail flying, and came down on its left side. For a few seconds the beast thrashed and kicked feebly, raising its head and snorting, and then it went limp and collapsed.

Nathaniel rode back toward the bull slowly, astounded he had survived, feeling keenly thrilled at their success. He stared at his uncle, who was riding over, noting Zeke's beaming smile and gleaming eyes.

Any vestige of the former cultured New Yorker was gone. His features flushed from the stimulation of the pursuit, elated at the slaying of the bull, his long hair tousled, his face covered with dust, Ezekiel threw back his head and laughed uproariously. He indicated the buffalo with a jab of his Hawken while looking at Nathaniel. "Ain't this the life, nephew! Out here, a man can *be* a man!"

"Provided he lives long enough."

The comment caused Zeke to laugh even harder.

# Chapter Sixteen

The next couple of weeks passed without any life-threatening incident occurring.

Ezekiel skillfully guided them on a northwesternly bearing, going from one watercourse to another. He seemed to know the location of every stream, river, and spring on their route. Game at times was scarce, but they never went hungry thanks to the buffalo meat Zeke had carved from the bull and dried.

Nathaniel used the opportunity to question his uncle more about the wildlife on the plains and in the mountains, as well as to elicit information about the various Indian tribes inhabiting the country. When they stopped to rest the horses or eat he would invariably practice with his Hawken, and he became quite adept at hitting small targets, such as clumps of earth or thin twigs stripped from the brush, at considerable distances. His best shot, though, entailed the downing of an antelope at 150 yards. He killed the animal with one shot through the head, and Zeke praised him highly.

Three times they came across Indian sign. Each time Zeke examined the ground carefully and announced that the sign was a day or two old. He taught Nathaniel the basics of reading tracks, of judging the weight from the depth of the impression and determining the age by the consistency of the soil and the degree of erosion.

One night, eight days after the buffalo chase, a strange incident transpired that Nathaniel would have reason to recall and regret later. They were seated around their fire, and Ezekiel was discoursing on the relative beauty of the women in the various Indians tribes, when he abruptly ceased speaking and straightened. "Did you hear that?"

"What?" Nathaniel responded, tensing, his right hand creeping to his Hawken.

"I don't know. A faint noise."

"What did it sound like?"

"Like the snap of a twig, only different."

"I didn't hear anything unusual."

Ezekiel stood and scanned the prairie to the southeast. "I'm sure I heard it."

Puzzled, Nathaniel also stood, his rifle at his waist. They heard so many sounds at any given time of the day: the cries of birds, including the piercing calls of certain hawks; the growls and snarls of the predators, including grizzlies and panthers; the howling and yipping of wolves and coyotes; the whistles and chattering of ground squirrels and prairie dogs; and, infrequently, the far-off war whoop of an Indian. In addition, at times the wind intensified and rustled the grass and the tumbleweeds. So why would Zeke become concerned at the snap of a mere twig?

"I must be getting jumpy in my old age," Zeke joked, and sat back down.

Eager to learn more about the Indian women his uncle had known, Nathaniel sank onto the ground, forgetting about the queer noise. The next day, though, he noticed that Zeke kept looking to the southeast, as if there might be someone or something out there, but Zeke never expressed any undue concern. Nathaniel dismissed the matter as unimportant.

Days later one of the most exciting events of the whole trip took place.

They came within sight of the Rocky Mountains.

Zeke spied them first, and pointed with his right hand. "There they are, nephew. The top of the world."

Squinting, Nathaniel shielded his eyes from the sun with his right palm and gazed at the distant peaks. Silhouetted on the far horizon, the mountains at first resembled low-flying clouds. As they trekked westward the range grew in size and grandeur, each peak acquiring an individuality of its very own, a unique, stark symmetry onto itself.

Ezekiel picked up the pace. They reached a shallow river and followed the waterway across the last stretch of plain to the foothills bordering the towering Rockies.

Never in his wildest imaginings had Nathaniel envisioned the mountains would be so awesome. The tallest of the peaks reared many thousands of feet into the air and were shrouded in caps of white snow. One of the mountains, in particular, the highest of the lot, looked like the father of all mountains, its lofty summit visible for dozens of miles out on the plains. The upper third of its towering slopes were covered in a mantle of white, layered with more snow than any other mountain. Another slightly smaller peak stood close by. Gazing at the highest mountain in reverent admiration, Nathaniel said softly, "I had no idea."

Zeke nodded. "It's beautiful, isn't it?"

"Does the tall one have a name?"

"A lot of the trappers and traders have taken to calling it Long's Peak after that crazy fellow who headed the Yellowstone Expedition."

The name jarred a memory. Nathaniel recalled reading about the Yellowstone Expedition of 1819 and 1820 while still in school. The leader had been a military man, a Major Stephen Long, and the press had reported extensively on his observations and conclusions regarding the plains. "Major Long? Why was he crazy?"

"I heard tell that the idiot claimed the prairies were unfit for settlement, that he called the country we just passed through the Great American Desert."

Nathaniel nodded. "I saw that on a map."

"The man didn't know what he was talking about."

"But you'd have to admit it would be difficult for farmers to make a living on the prairie. The soil isn't rich enough to support crops or livestock."

Zeke snorted. "Tell that to the millions of buffalo."

They rode higher, climbing deeper into the foothills, and the going was not as rough as Nathaniel anticipated would be the case. Game, particularly deer and elk, abounded. The hills became steeper. They skirted the higher peaks and loftier bluffs. After 12 miles of arduous travel they passed through a broad opening between two mountain ridges, and there below them, extending for many miles, lay a large valley replete with ample timber and meandering watercourses and rife with wildlife. The valley was almost completely ringed by mountains and hills. Long's Peak was now southwest of their location.

"As far as I know, nephew, no white men other than you, me, and Shakespeare have ever set foot in this valley," Zeke mentioned with pride in his tone, as if he had discovered a natural jewel others had missed.

"Is your cabin in this valley?" Nathaniel inquired.

Zeke started forward. "On the other side of the lake."

"What lake?"

"You'll see in a bit."

They descended to the valley floor, and once clear of the forest they had an unobstructed view for miles.

Nathaniel spied the large lake, toward which they rode rapidly, and he marveled at the profusion of wild fowl. Ducks, geese, gulls, and brants, among others, crowded the water to such an extent they appeared to barely have room to flap their wings. He saw a herd of blacktail deer to the south, and soaring high in the azure sky were several eagles and hawks. "This is a Garden of Eden," he breathed in fascination.

Ezekiel was studying his nephew intently. "I was hoping you'd like it."

"Does Shakespeare live here too?"

Zeke shook his head. "He's my nearest neighbor. His cabin is about twenty-five miles north of here."

"What about Indians?"

"You already know about the Cheyennes. They tend to stick to the prairie where most of the buffalo are found. Another tribe you're bound to meet are the Arapahos, the dog-eaters. They live on the plains too, but you'll find them hunting game in the foothills quite often. Their territory is just north of the Cheyenne hunting ground. The two tribes get along like two peas in a pod. They have an alliance. If you make an enemy of the Cheyenne, then you become an enemy of the Arapaho," Zeke detailed, then frowned. "The Cheyenne and the Arapaho will leave you alone. It's the Utes you have to worry about."

"Are they the ones who live on the west slope of the Rockies?"

Zeke nodded. "And the central Rockies. They've been at war with the Cheyenne and the Arapaho for decades. And the Utes will kill any white man they come across. Mark my words, nephew. Never trust a Ute. If you see one, shoot first and admire his buckskins later. I doubt if they'll ever learn to live at peace with anyone, let alone us whites."

"Have you had run-ins with them?"

"I've been obliged to kill about fifteen."

Nathaniel's eyebrow arched. "Fifteen?"

"Which is why they tend to leave me alone. A few years back they sent a war party to wipe me out. I was lucky. Shakespeare was paying a visit. I took an arrow in the thigh, and he pulled me into the cabin to safety. Those red devils tried every trick they could think of to force us out, even setting fire to my cabin, but our rifles taught them the error of their ways." Zeke chuckled. "I haven't seen hide nor hair of them varmints since."

"They'll be back one day," Nathaniel predicted.

"You think so, Mister Indian Expert?"

"Would you let it rest if you were them?"

Ezekiel regarded his relative thoughtfully and smiled. "No, I wouldn't. You're learning, Nathaniel. You'll make a great mountain man."

"I'll be back in civilization in a year, remember? I doubt anyone will ever know I was here."

Zeke did not respond. He pursed his lips and rode along the south shore of the lake, musing.

"Why did you call the Arapahos the dog eaters?" Nathaniel inquired out of curiosity.

"Because they eat dogs, nephew. They consider dog meat a real delicacy. They'll fatten their mongrels until the dogs are plump as a buffalo, then butcher them and have a fine meal."

Nathaniel scrunched up his nose at the idea of eating a dog. "Have you ever eaten dog meat?"

"On several occasions. If you ever visit an Arapaho camp, they'll likely offer you some. You'll insult them if you refuse."

"Remind me to never visit an Arapaho camp."

Zeke laughed. "If you stay out here long enough, you'll get over your finicky stomach."

"If you say so."

"Just don't take to eating people."

"Now you're joshing me."

"Nope. There are some folks who think human flesh is downright tasty. If you ever meet up with Old Bill, watch your hide."

"Who is he?"

"Old Bill Williams. He's a weird one. Lives all alone somewhere way up in the Rockies, but he comes down every now and then to socialize. You might bump into him at a rendezvous."

"And he eats people?"

"So they say."

"Surely you don't believe the stories?"

"I wouldn't, except for a little fact."

"What's that?"

"I had a talk with Old Bill two years ago, and I asked him point-blank if the tales were true, if he was partial to human flesh."

Nathaniel leaned forward, half expecting this to be another of Zeke's wild yarns. "And?"

"He looked me right in the eye and smacked his lips, then cackled like he was out of his mind. I believe the stories, and you'd be well advised to do the same."

Cannabalism? Nathaniel thought the very idea repugnant. He shook his head, stared ahead, and saw the cabin, a low log structure situated approximately 40 feet from the west end of the sparkling lake. He glanced to the north and spotted a river flowing into the lake, and traced the course of the river back into the higher country to the west.

"There's where I hang my leggings."

"How long have you lived there?"

"I built the place about five years ago."

"And you've lived there all alone?"

"Do you remember those Indian women I was telling you about?"

"Of course."

"Three of them were my wives, and they lived there in my cabin with me for a season or two of trapping."

"You have three wives!" Nathaniel exclaimed.

"Had, nephew. Had. And I didn't have them all at once, either. I haven't gone Indian that much," Zeke said, smirking. "I usually buy a wife at the rendezvous, keep her for a year, then take her back to her tribe to sell her once the attraction wears off."

Nathaniel almost reined up. "You *buy* your wives?"

"Of course. Why get hitched for the long haul when you can dally for the short term, if you get my drift."

"How can you *buy* a woman?"

"It's easy. A lot of Indians show up at the rendezvous, and they're more than happy to sell their women to whoever wants them. The ugly ones are right cheap, but the pretty ones will cost you a couple of horses, a gun with powder and ball, and a half-dozen pounds of beans or some whiskey. I know one joker who paid two thousand dollars in beaver skins for a chief's daughter. Talk about overpriced goods!" He chuckled.

Nathaniel was dazed. It never occurred to him that Indian women could be bought, could be paid for much like those slaves he had seen. The practice went against the moral fiber of his being. He stared at his uncle, amazed again at the uncanny transformation his uncle had undergone since leaving St. Louis. Zeke's outlook on life, his mannerisms, even his speech had slowly altered, as if St. Louis had temporarily drawn the old Ezekiel King to the surface and now the wilderness had reclaimed the man who had been molded in its own image.

"Here we are," Zeke announced, halting within five yards of the cabin door, which stood slightly ajar. "That's odd. I distinctly remember closing that door. I hope Silver Tip did't get in there or my goods will be in a shambles."

"Silver Tip?"

"A grizzly that lives in these parts. I've tried to kill him several times, but he's been too slippery for me," Zeke said, dismounting.

"How would a grizzly get in a locked door?"

"This isn't New York, nephew. Out here folks don't have to worry about locking—" Zeke began, then suddenly froze, staring at the cabin wall.

Nathaniel gazed in the same direction, at the logs to the left of the door, and saw it.

A tomahawk was imbedded in the wall.

"Utes!" Zeke declared.

# Chapter Seventeen

Nathaniel quickly dropped to the ground and scanned the valley. "Do you think they're still around?"

"I don't see any fresh sign," Zeke said. "I've been gone for months. They probably came to scalp me, then left this message when they found I wasn't home." He walked to the cabin, set down his rifle, and wrenched the tomahawk loose.

"Message?"

"No two tribes make their weapons alike," Zeke disclosed while inspecting the tomahawk. "This is definitely Ute. They wanted me to know they were here, to rub my nose in it, to show they're not afraid of me and to let me know they'll be back."

"Why didn't they burn your cabin?"

"This is personal between them and me. They want my hair hanging in one of their lodges. Maybe they figured I'd leave if they razed the cabin. I don't know."

They cautiously edged to the doorway. Zeke shoved the heavy door inward and they peered inside.

"Damn!"

"What a mess," Nathaniel commented, eyeing the

ransacked interior. Furniture had been broken. Blankets had been ripped to shreds. Pots and pans were scattered about, and numerous personal effects had been shattered to bits.

"They'll pay for this," Zeke vowed. He entered and kicked angrily at a busted chair. "I made that myself."

"We'll have this cleaned up in no time," Nathaniel said.

Ezekiel scowled. "I don't mind the mess so much. I can always replace the things the vermin broke. But they took all the meat I had cut and dried."

"What do you want me to do?"

"Tie up the horses. We'll tidy the cabin, unpack, and go fishing in the lake. You've never tasted fish so good as the trout in these mountains."

Nathaniel nodded and went to turn when a horrifying thought struck him. "The treasure!" he blurted anxiously.

"What about it?" Zeke replied, bending down to pick up the leg from a smashed table.

"Did the Utes find your treasure?"

"No."

"But you haven't checked."

"The treasure isn't in the cabin," Zeke assured him. "I know they didn't find it."

"When will I get to see it?"

"Soon enough. Now get busy with those horses."

Nathaniel strolled to his mare, mystified by his uncle's nonchalant attitude. If *he* had a treasure cached nearby, it would be the first thing he checked. A squirrel chattered at him from a nearby pine tree, and he halted to gaze at the beautiful scenery all around him. This was so different from New York City. He remembered the sooty air, the crowds, and the grimy streets, and slowly shook his head. Perhaps Zeke was right. Compared to the pristine purity of the virgin wilderness, city life seemed unnatural. All those people crammed into a limited space, fouling the air with soot and the ground with their excrement, seemed vile and gross. Cities were breeding grounds for rats of the four-legged and the two-legged variety.

But out here!

He inhaled deeply, invigorated by the crisp air, and stared at the snow-capped peaks in the distance. A man could easily become addicted to such splendor, he mused. No wonder his uncle had never returned, and how wrong his father had been to condemn Zeke for choosing to live in harmony with Nature. Which, after all, *was* more natural? To live and work in cramped confines, to have walls and buildings limit the view, to breathe fouled air and eat overly salted meat? Or to have the far horizon be your wall and the sky your ceiling, to breathe in air as fresh as that on the day the world was created, and to eat the still-warm flesh of an animal recently slain?

Nathaniel grinned and took hold of the mare's reins. If he didn't know better, he'd swear he was beginning to thoroughly enjoy the wilderness life. If he wasn't careful, he might wind up like his uncle.

The thought made him laugh.

That afternoon, after the cabin had been cleaned out and their provisions stored inside, they went down to the lake to fish. Zeke constructed a pair of makeshift poles from the thin limbs of a tree. Within half an hour they had seven large trout on the bank.

"Tomorrow we'll go after an elk," Zeke mentioned as they ambled toward the cabin. He carried his rifle in his right hand, their poles in his left. "We'll gorge ourselves and dry some of the meat before we head out for the rendezvous."

"When do I get to see the treasure?" Nathaniel asked, hefting the string of fish in his left hand. Slanted over his right shoulder was his Hawken.

Ezekiel looked at his nephew. "Is that all you think about?"

"Wouldn't you if you were in my shoes?"

"I reckon I would," Zeke conceded, his features clouding. "Very well. Tomorrow morning I'll show you the treasure."

Nathaniel beamed. He could hardly wait! At last he would have the wealth he needed to woo Adeline properly! Elated, he gazed idly at the cabin, and as he did he heard an unusual swishing noise, and then a pronounced thump and a grunt. He glanced at his uncle and instantly halted, transfixed by the sight of a lance protruding from Zeke's chest.

Ezekiel was standing stock still, regarding the lance in bewilderment, his shoulders sagging. "Damn! Not again!" he exclaimed, and fell to his knees, releasing the poles but not his rifle.

"Uncle Zeke!" Nathaniel cried. He dropped the fish and looped his left arm around his uncle's shoulders.

"Get us inside, quick," Zeke urged.

Nathaniel scanned the forest, expecting a lance or an arrow to streak out of nowhere at him. He detected movement in the brush to the left of the cabin, approximately 20 feet from the door, and he let go of Zeke, whipped the Hawken up, and fired at a vague figure in the shadows. The figure promptly vanished.

"Inside," Zeke reiterated weakly. "Hurry, nephew."

The hair at the nape of his neck prickling, Nathaniel supported his uncle with his left arm and together they made for the shelter of the log structure. Zeke walked unsteadily and breathed loudly. Constantly surveying the woods for Indians, dreading another attack before they could reach safety, Nathaniel resisted an urge to dash inside. He assisted Zeke in reaching the cabin, and once they were there he lowered his uncle to the floor and immediately closed the door.

"I sure am having a pitiful run of luck," Zeke quipped, sitting stooped over. The lance had passed completely through his body, entering just an inch to the right of his sternum and exiting low down on his back, above the hip bone.

"The Utes must have been waiting for you to return," Nathaniel mentioned, kneeling next to Zeke.

"It's not the Utes."

"What?"

Zeke bobbed his chin lower. "This lance isn't a Ute lance."

"Then who—?" Nathaniel began.

"It's a Kiowa lance."

"But you told me the Kiowa don't range this far," Nathaniel commented while examining the shaft. He remembered how the Cheyenne, White Eagle, had extracted the arrow, and he reached for the lance, intending to do the same.

"Don't bother," Zeke said.

"But we can't leave it in."

"Check the window," Zeke advised.

Nathaniel propped his rifle against the wall and took his uncle's Hawken. He stepped to the only window, located to the right of the door. There was no glass, but a deerskin flap had been tacked to the top, rolled up, and then tied to afford a passage for the breeze. Inching his head to the sill, he peeked outside and saw only the trees, the lake, and the fowl. "I don't see anyone," he whispered.

"The savage is playing a game with us."

"Who is?"

"Thunder Rider."

"Do you mean he followed us all the way here?"

"That'd be my guess, nephew."

"But White Eagle and those other Cheyenne went after him."

"He got away from them."

Nathaniel still couldn't believe that the Kiowa warrior had trailed them so far. "How could he follow us without you spotting him?"

"He's an Indian, Nate, not a clumsy white man like Gant and those others."

Perplexed, Nathanial scurried back to his uncle. "But why would he come all this way? Why didn't he ambush us earlier?"

"I don't know why he waited so long. Maybe he felt he couldn't get close enough to us on the prairie. Or maybe he just wanted to learn where we were headed," Zeke said. "But I do know he's out for revenge. We shamed him, and he won't rest until he's taken our hair."

Nathaniel stared at the lance, alarmed at the red stain

developing on his uncle's shirt. "How do I remove the damn thing?"

"You don't."

"We've got to do something," Nathaniel insisted. "Tell me how to remove the lance."

Ezekiel looked into his nephew's eyes. "There's no need," he responded, the words barely audible.

"Why not?" Nathaniel queried, instinctively sensing the answer, filled with fear at what his uncle might say next. ·

"I'm dying, Nate."

The statement resounded in Nathaniel's mind with all the force of a thunderclap, and he stared at his uncle in disbelief. "You can't die."

"We all do eventually," Zeke said, and gave a wan smile.

"But you don't know for a fact that you're dying. If I take out the lance and dress the wound, you could live."

"I know it, Nate. I can feel it. I'm all torn up inside. I'm leaking like a sieve."

"You don't know that!" Nathaniel insisted, a tinge of desperation to his voice.

"I do. It feels like I have an itch inside, only I can't scratch it."

Nathaniel swallowed hard and felt tears in his eyes. "You can't die! I won't accept it!" He glanced wildly about the cabin. "There must be *something* I can do!"

"There is."

"What?" Nathaniel queried eagerly, leaning forward. "I'll do anything. What do you want done?"

"I want you to take Thunder Rider's hair."

Nathaniel recoiled. "You want me to scalp him?"

"Yep. But kill the son of a bitch first. He might object, otherwise," Zeke said, and grinned. Suddenly he coughed violently and put his left hand over his mouth. When the fit subsided and he removed his hand, both his lips and his palm were covered with blood.

"Dear God!" Nathaniel declared. "This can't be happening."

"Get a grip on yourself, Grizzly Killer," Zeke stated.

"This is survival, remember? Either you kill the Kiowa or he'll kill you."

"I won't leave your side."

"You don't have any choice. Listen, Nate. Thunder Rider was leading that war party. When a warrior leads a raid and doesn't lose a man, he's honored by his tribe. If the war party suffers a loss, though, that's considered bad medicine. Thunder Rider must avenge the warriors we killed and take our scalps back to his tribe to erase his shame."

"He won't live that long," Nathaniel vowed gruffly.

"That's the King spirit," Zeke said, and erupted into another fit of coughing. Blood spilled from the corners of his mouth and he gasped for air.

Terrified of losing his uncle, Nathaniel placed his left hand on Zeke's shoulder, wishing there was something he could do to relieve Zeke's suffering. "Please, no," he said.

A shadow flitted across the window, momentarily blocking off the sunlight.

Nathaniel tensed, gripped the Hawken in both hands, and moved toward the window. He had to be extremely wary. The Kiowa warrior was out there somewhere, waiting for him to make a mistake. He had to remember everything Zeke had taught him and finish off the warrior quickly. The sooner Thunder Rider was dead, the sooner he could tend to his uncle. He glanced out the window but saw no one.

There was only one way to get the job done.

Looking one last time at Zeke, who had closed his eyes and was wheezing, Nathaniel walked to the door. If he stayed inside, the warrior would simply wait him out or set fire to the cabin. He had to go out, to meet Thunder Rider in the open, to draw the Indian to him.

"Nate?" Zeke said huskily, his eyes still shut.

"I'm here," Nathaniel replied.

A protracted sigh issued from Zeke's crimson flecked lips. "I'm so—sorry."

"Don't talk. Save your breath. I'll be right back," Nathaniel stated. He faced the door, squared his shoulders, and gripped the latch.

"So sorry," Zeke repeated.

Nathaniel opened the door and pulled it inward, standing behind the wooden panel for protection, scrutinizing the terrain between the cabin and the lake. Where would Thunder Rider be hiding? In the trees on either side most likely, he deduced, and wondered if the warrior possessed another lance or bow. He heard a faint scratching noise and stiffened. What was that?

The scratching ceased.

"Never expected this," Zeke said.

Girding his courage, Nathaniel slipped outside and flattened against the outer wall. The air felt cool and clammy on his face, and he realized he'd been sweating profusely. He looked to the right and the left, cocked the Hawken, and edged to the southeast corner.

Somewhere in the forest a bird was singing.

The ducks and geese were swimming sedately on the lake.

Off to the south stood a solitary black-tailed doe.

Who would guess that death lurked in the trees? Nathaniel thought, then frowned at his lapse in concentration. To survive he must focus all of his attention on the present. He must be guided by his eyes and ears and act on impulse rather than reason.

Where was Thunder Rider?

Nathaniel studied the forest, checking every tree, every boulder, any place the warrior might be hiding. Another thought occurred to him and gave him pause.

What if Thunder Rider had obtained a rifle?

He dismissed the idea as unlikely. If the Kiowa had a rifle, Thunder Rider would have used it instead of a lance. Or so he hoped. After a minute, satisfied the warrior was not on that side of the cabin, Nathaniel moved to the northeast corner. Again he scrutinized the tall timber, and again he failed to detect the Indian.

A loud groan came from inside the cabin.

Nathaniel frowned and stepped back toward the doorway, thinking of Zeke alone and in exquisite agony. Uncertainty seized him, and he wavered between staying outside and searching for the warrior or going in to comfort his uncle.

Distracted by his thoughts, he scarcely noticed when a few pieces of dirt or splinters of wood fell onto his shoulders. Not until a flake landed on his nose did he finally look up, and by then it was too late.

Because he had found Thunder Rider.

Uttering a piercing screech, a knife clutched in his right hand, the Kiowa warrior launched himself from the roof.

# Chapter Eighteen

Nathaniel tried to bring the Hawken to bear, sweeping the barrel upward, but the Indian's hurtling form struck the rifle and sent it flying even as Thunder Rider landed on top of his shoulders, driving Nathaniel forward, away from the cabin. He felt the weight of the warrior on his back, felt a hand brutally yank on his hair, and the force of the impact knocked him to his knees. He arced his body down, lowering his forehead to the ground, attempting to flip the Indian off. He succeeded.

Thunder Rider hit the grass and rolled, displaying the reflexes of a panther. He leaped to his feet, still brandishing the knife, a wicked grin twisting his countenance, apparently confident of victory.

A shade slower in rising, Nathaniel clawed for his right pistol. His fingers were just closing on the grip when the warrior came at him again, slashing that gleaming blade back and forth, forcing him to retreat and to release the pistol or have his hand sliced open.

Thunder Rider vented a war whoop and sprang.

Frantically backpedaling to evade the knife, Nathaniel abruptly bumped into the cabin wall. He started to dodge to the right, intending to dart inside, but somehow the warrior anticipated his move and skipped between the door and him. Frustrated, he retreated toward the northeast corner, never turning his back to the Indian for fear of being knifed. He managed only four strides when the unforeseen transpired.

He tripped.

Nathaniel felt an object under his left heel and began to lose his balance. He threw his arms out, flapping them in an effort to stay upright, and in that instant when he was most vulnerable, the warrior pounced.

Thunder Rider lowered his head and charged, his left hand going for his victim's throat, his right arm swinging the knife in a vicious arc.

Flailing recklessly as he fell, Nathaniel blocked the knife swing. But he couldn't prevent the warrior's left hand from clamping onto his throat, and he landed on his back with the Kiowa astride his chest and the knife already spearing in at his neck. His eyes wide, he snatched at the Indian's wrist and held on for precious life, all the while prying at the fingers on his throat, trying to breathe.

A feral gleam lit up the warrior's eyes. His maniacal thirst for revenge had supplanted all conscious thought. He lived only to kill the men who had slain his fellows, and he would achieve his goal or perish in the attempt.

Nathaniel experienced more difficulty in breathing. He couldn't tear the Indian's fingers from his throat, and the razor point of the knife was slowly descending closer and closer. If he didn't break free in the next few seconds, he would die. And so would Zeke if he wasn't already dead.

Ezekiel!

The thought of his dying, helpless uncle spurred Nathaniel into action. He bucked and thrashed, then drove his right knee up into the warrior's back. Once. Twice. And again for good measure, and on the third blow the Kiowa's visage contorted in pain and Thunder Rider threw himself to the right. Nathaniel heaved to his feet, his left hand finding the left pistol and drawing as he rose.

The warrior also leaped erect.

Nathaniel pointed the pistol at Thunder Rider and cocked the hammer. He saw the warrior's look of stunned surprise, and he allowed himself the luxury of a smile, knowing he had won, knowing he was about to pay the Kiowa back in kind for Zeke. And then he squeezed the trigger.

Nothing happened.

Except for the ticking sound of the flint, absolutely nothing happened.

The pistol had misfired.

Thunder Rider vented a triumphant scream and closed in again, batting the pistol from his foe's hand with the blade of his knife.

Nathaniel recovered quickly and took several swift steps toward the northeast corner. His gaze alighted on the rifle, lying at the base of the cabin wall, and he angled for it, diving and gripping the barrel in both hands. He twisted onto his side and saw the warrior already in midair, that glistening blade extended, and he did the only thing he could. He swung the Hawken like a club, whipping the heavy stock in a circle, catching the Indian full on the face, the wood crushing Thunder Rider's nostrils and the force of the blow knocking the Indian to the ground. Nathaniel adjusted his grip and pressed the rifle to his right shoulder, about to fire.

The Kiowa warrior rolled to the right, then surged to his feet and did the unexpected. He threw his knife.

Nathaniel jerked his head to the right, but it wasn't enough to completely dodge the weapon. The blade bit into his left temple and sliced open a shallow groove, causing a lancing pang in his head. He ignored the feeling and sighted on the Indian's head, smack between the eyes.

Thunder Rider shrieked and attacked one more time.

Cooly, calmly, Nathaniel fired, wondering in the back of his mind if using the rifle like a club might have damaged the gun in some way, if it would misfire as the pistol had done. He needn't have worried. The Hawken belched smoke and lead, and never in all his life had Nathaniel heard any sound as sweet as the sharp retort of the rifle.

The ball struck the warrior at the top of the nose and

snapped his head back, spinning him in his tracks. He stopped and blinked once or twice, as if astounded at the outcome, and slowly sank to his knees, then pitched onto his stomach, his arms outflung.

Nathaniel took a deep breath, striving to soothe his suddenly fluttering nerves. Now that the fight was over, his blood seemed to be racing through his body of its own volition. He stared at the lifeless warrior and dropped the Hawken, his hands trembling.

What was wrong with him?

Why couldn't he concentrate?

An unexpected exhaustion made Nathaniel slump onto his back for a few seconds. He stared at the blue sky and spotted an eagle soaring far, far overhead. Putting his palms on the ground, he pushed himself up and stood. His knees were unaccountably wobbly and he leaned on the cabin for support.

A pool of blood was forming under Thunder Rider's head.

Nathaniel gazed at the warrior for a full minute. He'd killed again. How many did that make now? There had been the man with Gant at the Republican River. There had been that Indian during the battle on the hill. Maybe several Indians. So he'd slain at least three men, perhaps more, since leaving St. Louis. To his pleasant surprise, he did not feel any degree of remorse this time. Thunder Rider had needed killing.

It was as simple as that.

His strength returning, Nathaniel pivoted and hastened into the cabin. He almost cried out when he saw his uncle lying on the floor.

Ezekiel had collapsed onto his left side, his hands clasping the lance. Blood caked his chin and neck and coated his hands.

"Zeke!" Nathaniel shouted, reaching his uncle in a bound and kneeling alongside him.

There was no response.

Nathaniel leaned over and gingerly touched his uncle's chest. Relief brought moisture to his eyes when Zeke's eyelids fluttered.

"Nate? Is that you?"

"It's me."

"Did you kill him?"

"He won't be bothering us ever again."

Zeke coughed lightly. "Where's the scalp you promised me?"

"I—I haven't taken it yet."

"No hurry, I reckon," Zeke said. His voice rasped when he spoke, and tiny red bubbles formed on his lips.

Overcome with emotion at the impending loss of his uncle, Nathaniel placed his right hand on Zeke's shoulder. "Please don't die."

"I don't have much choice in the matter."

"There must be *something* I can do!"

"There is. Take me outdoors."

"What?"

Zeke twisted his head a few inches, grimacing with the effort. "I don't want to die in a building. Please, Nate. Carry me outside."

A knot seemed to have formed in Nathaniel's throat. He nodded and eased his arms under his uncle, then straightened, his face turning red from the strain, trying to be as gentle as possible. "Where outside?"

"Anywhere I can see the mountains."

Nathaniel conveyed his uncle out the door and several yards into the open, then tenderly deposited Ezekiel on the cool grass, laying the frontiersman down on his left side so Zeke could gaze to the south and see Long's Peak.

"Thank you, nephew."

"Is there anything else I can do?"

"You can listen."

"Why don't you save your breath?" Nathaniel suggested, sinking onto his right knee.

"For what? Eternity?"

Nathaniel bowed his head.

"I have to tell you," Zeke said. "You need to know about the treasure."

"I don't care about the treasure now," Nathaniel stated, and he meant it. What did wealth matter when he was about to lose a man he had grown to deeply respect and love?

Zeke, strangely, smiled. "That's good. Because there isn't any."

"What?"

"There isn't any treasure, at least not in the way you think there is."

Confused, his brow furrowed, Nathaniel bent over his uncle, trying to read Zeke's expression. "I don't understand. You told me there's a treasure. And you had all those gold nuggets."

"If you trap beaver in these mountains long enough, you'll find a few nuggets too. As for the greatest treasure in the world, I've already shared it with you."

"You have?"

"Look at those mountains," Zeke said, then added forcefully when his nephew didn't comply, "*Look* at them, Nate!"

Nathaniel stared at the majestic peaks, confounded by the revelation, at a loss for words.

"Now look at the lake," Zeke directed. "Do it."

Shifting on his knee, Nathaniel gazed at the sparkling water.

"Take a good look at this valley, Nate. Look at the wildlife, at the deer and the elk and the other game. Think about the fact that all this is now yours. My cabin, my rifle, my clothes, everything I leave to you," Zeke said. "And I leave you with one more thing. The greatest treasure in the world. The treasure that I found when I came out to the Rockies. The treasure I wanted to share with the only relative I give a damn about. The treasure I wanted to share with you, Nate."

Nathaniel looked down. "What treasure?"

"Freedom."

Dazed, Nathaniel shook his head and pressed his right hand to his forehead. "You brought me all the way out here to give me something I already had?"

"Did you? Do you call sitting behind a desk all day, scribbling numbers with a pencil and taking orders from a man who probably considers himself your better, *freedom*? Do you call marrying a woman who is more interested in money than in your happiness *freedom*? Do you call letting your life be run by others *freedom*?''

"But it's not as if I was in chains."

"There are visible and invisible chains, Nate. You told me about those slaves you saw. They wore visible chains. But you were wearing the worst kind. You were wearing invisible chains, the chains of laws and rules and regulations imposed by others who want to control your life for their own selfish ends," Zeke stated passionately, and the exertion cost him. His chin sagged and he groaned.

Nathaniel rested his hand on his uncle's arm. "I don't know what to say."

Zeke's lips barely moved. "Tell me you'll stay out here. Live in my cabin. Learn to trap. Make your mark in the world, but do it your way."

"I don't know how to trap."

"Shakespeare will teach you."

"How do I find him?"

"He should be here in a few days. We were going to the rendezvous together. He'll take you."

"But what if I want to go home?"

"You can trust Shakespeare, Nate," Zeke said, as if he hadn't heard.

"What if the Utes come before he shows up?"

"Then show them that you're a man. Show them that you're the lord of this valley, that you're the king of the mountains." Zeke grinned, then gasped.

"Oh, God, Uncle Zeke!"

Ezekiel glanced up, his eyes startlingly clear. "You're a man, now. You have to give up your boyish ways. In the city you can still be a boy at nineteen. Out here you can't. You're Nate King, free trapper, mountain man, and the master of your own destiny." He inhaled noisily and struggled to speak one more time. "I've done all I can. The rest is up to you. Make me proud, Nate. I'm going to meet the Eternal."

"Zeke!"

A soft whisper came from Ezekiel King's lips. He stiffened, straightening to his full length, and then went limp, his head settling on the green carpet underneath his cheek, his eyes closing, a curious smile creasing his lips.

Far overhead the eagle soared.

# Epilogue

He rode into the valley through the broad opening between the ridges, sitting astride a white horse, a Hawken cradled in his big arms. His shoulder-length hair, his beard, and his mustache were all a striking white, his eyes a sea blue. He wore buckskins and a brown beaver hat, and slanted across his chest were his powder horn and his bullet pouch.

The valley appeared tranquil.

Accustomed to the path he followed, he rode down to the valley floor and toward the lake teeming with geese and ducks. Beyond the lake stood the familiar cabin, and the rider smiled in anticipation. He goaded his horse to go a little faster, taking the south bank, watching gray smoke curl upward from the narrow chimney. Not until he was 20 yards from his destination did he spy the freshly dug grave and reined up.

The low mound of earth was situated ten yards to the south of the cabin, in an open area.

The rider took a firmer grip of his rifle and rode closer. That was when he saw the Indian and his eyes widened.

Someone had placed the body 30 yards away, simply

dumped it on the hard ground and left it there to rot. The warrior lay on his back. He had been scalped.

"Can I help you?"

The hard tone drew the rider around to the north. A man was standing at the northeast corner, a rifle in his hands, a man with green eyes and black hair, wearing buckskins and a red Mackinaw coat. "Howdy, neighbor," the rider said in a friendly fashion. "Who might you be?"

"You're the one who's trespassing in my valley," the man responded. "Who are you?"

"Folks hereabouts call me Shakespeare."

"You're Shakespeare?" the man in red replied, and took several strides forward. "Zeke told me to expect you."

"And who are you?"

"His nephew."

Shakespeare scarcely concealed his surprise. "*You're* Nathaniel?"

"*Nate*. Nate King."

"Well, I'm right pleased to meet you." Shakespeare glanced at the grave. "Is that who I think it is?"

"Zeke was killed by a Kiowa."

Sadness etched the rugged mountain man's features. "Alas, poor Ezekiel. I knew him well. A fellow of infinite jest, of most excellent fancy; he bore me on his back a thousand times."

"What?"

The mountain man stared at the man in red. "That's Shakespeare, Nate. Of a sort, anyway. And that's why folks call me by that name." He reached back and thumped a rolled blanket tied behind his saddle. "I never go anywhere without my book on old William S."

"I'm pleased to make your acquaintance," Nate said. "Why don't you climb down and share some elk meat with me?"

"I don't mind if I do," Shakespeare answered. He rode up to the cabin and dismounted.

"We can leave for the rendezvous in the morning," Nate stated.

"You want to go to the rendezvous?"

"I do. My uncle told me I can trust you, that you'll teach me everything I need to know."

The mountain man grinned. "It seems like I'm making it my life's business to teach Kings the facts of life."

"I already know them," Nate said, and motioned at the open door. "Come on in. I want you to tell me all about Zeke."

Shakespeare laughed. "That'd take a year."

"I have the time." Nate turned and entered the cabin.

Chuckling, Shakespeare took a step, about to go in, when his gaze fell on the scalp nailed to the front of the door, a scalp recently removed. He looked back at the dead Indian, then at the hair hanging in front of him. "What's this?" he asked.

The reply was a full ten seconds in coming.

"Nothing. Nothing at all."